THE BODY ON MOUNT ROYAL

BY THE SAME AUTHOR

The Crime on Cote des Neiges (1951)

Murder Over Dorval (1952)

The Body on Mount Royal

DAVID MONTROSE

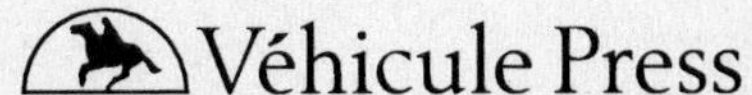

Published with the assistance of the Canada Council for the Arts, the Canada Book Fund of the Department of Canadian Heritage, and the Société de développement des entreprises culturelles du Québec (SODEC).

Cover design: David Drummond
Consulting editor: Brian Busby
Special assistance: Asa Boxer

Typeset in Minion by Simon Garamond
Printed by Marquis Printing Inc.

LIBRARY AND ARCHIVES CANADA CATALOGUING IN PUBLICATION

Montrose, David, 1920-1968
The body on Mount Royal / David Montrose ; introduction by Kevin Burton Smith.

(Ricochet books)
ORIGINALLY PUBLISHED: TORONTO : HARLEQUIN, 1953.
ISBN 978-1-55065-290-1

I TITLE. II. SERIES: RICOCHET BOOKS

PS8526.O593B63 2012 C813'.54 C2012-901921-6

Published by Véhicule Press, Montréal, Québec, Canada
www.vehiculepress.com

Distribution in Canada by LitDistCo
www.litdistco.ca

Distributed in the U.S. by Independent Publishers Group
www.ipgbook.com

Printed in Canada on recycled paper

INTRODUCTION

Pulp Fiction Chez Vous

Kevin Burton Smith

HERE WE ARE. Pulp fiction *chez nous*. As vivid as Raymond Chandler's Los Angeles, as Montreal as a quart of Molson.

But let's get this straight. This is not your Montréal.

This is not the vibrant, bike-friendly, earnestly tolerant multicultural city which has thrown open its arms to the world—a celebrated centre of education, arts and culture; an important hub of commerce and industry; a player in the fields of aerospace, finance, technology, design, film and world affairs; a city so elastically hip that it gave the world both Leonard Cohen and Arcade Fire, Michel Tremblay and Mordecai Richler, Cirque du soleil and Irving Layton, Joe Beef and the Montreal bagel.

No, this is another Montreal.

The Montreal of the 1950s. A wide-open city, the "Paris of the North," a city of churches and sin, known for its taverns and gambling joints, neon-lit cabarets featuring world class entertainment, dingy pool rooms and dingier blind pigs, late night bars and beautiful women, colourful underworld figures and a stench of corruption so entrenched that even Chandler, 3,000 miles away, considered Montreal "almost as crooked as we are."

This is the Montreal of man-about-town Al Palmer's *Montreal Confidential*, the tell-all 1950 paperback that promised "the low down on the big town."

This is the Montreal of perpetual mayor Camillien Houde; of perpetual provincial premier Maurice Duplessis; of Toe

Blake, Punch Imlach, Rocket Richard and Les Glorieux.

This is also very much the Montreal of Hugh MacLennan's *Two Solitudes*. Montrose's lack of acknowledgement of the French population of Montreal (not to mention some of his other less than enlightened views towards women and minorities) is pretty much par for the course, and pretty much nails the "two solitudes" mindset of the era—already disclaimed and apologized for in the introductions to the two previous Montrose books by my predecessors, Brian Busby and Michael Blair. In their way, however, the three novels are as honest and fair a depiction of a time and a place as anything Richler or Beauchemin or Tremblay ever penned. But of course this is not their Montreal, either. It is a Montreal, though, a real and vibrant Montreal, a Montreal where then as now people lived and worked and loved and died, pushed and pulled, divided and united by passions both real and imagined.

This is the Montreal of my father, who in 1953, the year in which *The Body on Mont Royal* was published, would have been a young man, just returned from Korea after serving in the Van Doos, dazzled by the bright lights and promise of a city laid open.

And it's the Montreal of private eye Russell Teed.

Russell Teed was created by David Montrose (real name: Charles Ross Graham). Graham was born in 1920 in New Brunswick and died in 1968 in Toronto. But in between, he lived for several years in Montreal, and during that time wrote the three novels featuring Teed: *The Crime on Cote des Neiges* (1951), *Murder Over Dorval* (1952) and the third and final volume that you now hold in your hands, *The Body on Mount Royal* (1953).

As you might guess from the violence contained within

the titles alone, Montrose was clearly a disciple of the hard-boiled school. His wise-cracking gumshoe was a righter of wrongs; a good man to call when you're in a bad jam; a seeker of truth and maybe even justice, going down those mean streets, neither tarnished nor afraid. But *les rues maudit* that Teed travelled were not the American alleys and avenues of Philip Marlowe's Los Angeles, Sam Spade's San Francisco or Mike Hammer's New York, but those of *notre ville*, from Craig Street (now rue St-Antoine) to the neon-lit Decarie Strip, from The Boulevard to Dorchester (now René-Lévesque).

And it wasn't street names alone that made Teed so distinctive—he truly was one of us; a *pure laine* Montrealer no matter where his creator may have been born.

Unlike his contemporaries, allies in the shamus game, Teed—in true Montreal fashion—did not necessarily drink alone. Over the course of three novels, he and his best buddy MacArnold, a "by-line bum" working for *The Montreal Clarion* and Teed's would-be Watson, put away an astounding amount of beer and other assorted alcoholic beverages, occasionally with the help of (often on-duty) Montreal homicide dick Raoul Framboise and other miscreants, while trying to sort out the mish-mash of lies, treachery, violence and jaw-dropping coincidence that were part and parcel of most hard-boiled plots of the time.

Sir Arthur Conan Doyle, not to mention Bob and Doug, would be proud.

A son of Westmount (although he's quick to point out not of its upper echelon), Teed drinks Molson and Dow (often ordered two quarts at a time) and likes cheese from Oka. He went to McGill, worked for a while as a reporter for the *Clarion*, one of the city's English-language dailies, and then went off to WWII for King and Country, where he saw more than enough of what men can do to other men.

Upon his return, he became a professional freelance investigator, setting up shop in the Canam Building across Dominion Square from the Sun Life Building, and specializing in white collar crime. As MacArnold explains it, Teed is:

> A private operative. Very big time. All sorts of contracts... mostly company work. Not the cases where the bookkeeper skips with a thousand iron men (but) the cases where the chairman of the board thinks the secretary-treasurer has been cooking the company balance sheet to buy himself a small republic in South America.

Seeking out and exposing financial shenanigans evidently pays well—Teed may not be rich, but he has a swinging little bachelor flat on Côte des Neiges, right near Westmount Boulevard and tools around town in a spiffy little Riley roadster (which he annoyingly calls Riley). Needless to say, he also enjoys the company of various beautiful women.

But somehow, despite his lofty and lucrative corporate work, Russ manages to get involved in some pretty down-and-dirty business. His cases may not have the most logical of solutions, and coincidence, happenstance and alcohol seem to be his chief deductive tools, but who cares? This truly is pulp fiction *chez nous*, warts and all.

And *The Body on Mount Royal* may be the best of the bunch.

The plot is certainly tighter than its predecessors, although that may not be saying much, but the stakes, both mortal and personal, are just a little bit higher. There's vengeance and blackmail and treachery, and more than enough action to keep things hopping. As well, the local colour is just a little bit more sharply rendered, as when Teed turns "poetic" (while sitting in the Stanley Street Tavern) about Montreal taverns with their "dark wood walls, smoked black from the fumes of a billion cigarettes" or when he offhandedly muses, while walking along with the wind rustling the leaves overhead on how "Montreal is a good city for trees."

I've read most of the Montreal pulp fiction novels of the era, the Douglas Sandersons, the early Brian Moores, Al Palmer's own *Sugar-Puss on Dorchester Street*, and Montrose definitely had—dare I say it?—a distinct voice. It was more wryly observant and cheeky than the sober-minded Brian Moore, and Teed's beer glass level view of our city recalled Chandler a little in his sense of place. Certainly, Montrose was more measured and grounded, and offered a much more vivid sense of community than Sanderson, whose desperate lone wolves seemed to be always on the verge of losing it—politically, emotionally, even psychologically. Sanderson was pulpier and darker—and messier. Montrose, I think, had higher aspirations. Or maybe not. Who knows?

None of the Teed novels ever made it to hardcover, and no respectable journal of the time reviewed paperbacks. The first two were published by White Circle, a British outfit, and the final one by Harlequin, back when the Winnipeg publisher still published all sorts of genre fiction.

And then, *rien...*

The Teed books didn't exactly set the world—or even Montreal—on fire. Montrose seems to have stepped out of the light. A chemical analyst, a lecturer and a freelance writer, he finally returned to fiction with one last novel, *Gambling With Fire*, in 1969. It was a crime novel set in Montreal, but it did not feature Teed. By the time it appeared on bookshelves, Montrose had already passed away, although the author's bio assured readers he was "living in Toronto."

Which, for a real Montrealer, just about sums it up. But now Véhicule Press, under their Ricochet imprint, has resurrected the entire Teed trilogy, finally adding some much needed pulpy fibre to our literary consciousness.

My dad would approve.

So, reach into your pocket and buy this book. Then head to your favourite tavern, pull up a wooden chair, order up a quart (or two) of Molson, and settle back. You're in for a good time.

Just remember, for the next few hundred pages, this isn't your Montreal.

It's Russell Teed's.

Bienvenue.

Kevin Burton Smith is the editor and founder of *The Thrilling Detective* Web Site: www.thrillingdetective.com.

Chapter One

YOU WANT TO KNOW about Montreal? Listen. I'll tell you.

The first anyone heard of Montreal, it was an Indian village called Hochelaga. The name has been changed a few times since then, but the place is still full of Indians. Low life, high life, all around the town, we got Indians. Not Red. White.

I could tell you about the high life, about the people who have homes beautiful as Forest Hill Villagers but instead of keeping them private castles, use them for only one thing—entertaining. The people who dine at La Maisonette Carol and Chez Ernest and Au Lutin qui Bouffe, and dance and drink in the Ritz Cafe or the Normandie or Le Pavillion. The people with Cadillac convertibles—Montreal is a city of convertibles, but a lot of them are Morris Minors.

I could tell you about them. But I have a hunch you want to hear about the people I know better, the ones I work among and get drunk with, and beat up or get beat up by. Sure, I know the rolling greenery of upper Westmount and the high square solemn houses of midtown Montreal's Square Mile, and the wide streets of Outremont with mansions set away back. But my name is Russell Teed. R. Teed, Private Investigator. I don't always like it, but I get involved in crimes. And I go where the criminals go.

I can take you to restaurants where you get a beautiful steak for four bits, and I can even tell you where they get the horses to cut up. I can stand you on a street corner where a man has never stood alone for five minutes without being approached by a pimp. I can get you a bottle, or a drink in a bar, at five in the morning if you won't tell the cops. And if you want to risk your roll at barbotte or crap or even, God save us, roulette, I can show you places that will cover your ten grand bet—and pay off if you win.

Montreal is a city with honest cops. But it's a big city with a tradition of Indian living, and there are places, there are places. I'll take you anywhere. I'll tell you anything you want to know. And I'll give you one piece of advice.

Don't walk alone on Mount Royal at night.

Maybe nothing will happen. Maybe you're big and brave. But a big, brave friend of mine looked awful funny without his wallet, wristwatch, glasses, pants, and false teeth. He lost them on top of Mount Royal and got in exchange a black eye and a broken jaw. And that's not all.

Once in a while the hugger-muggers get careless and hit too hard, and then in the morning somebody finds a body on Mount Royal. One particular body that was found there was the beginning of this story, though I didn't know it at the time. I'll tell you about him now, the way I heard about it myself, in the words the newspapers used the next day:

> "The brutally-beaten body of a man identified by police as Martin Chesterley, 53, 3975 McTavish St., was found at 6:45 a.m. near the summit of Mount Royal by James C. Montgomery, The Gordon Arms Apartment, Ridgewood Avenue.
>
> "Police said Chesterley had been dead for three to five hours when found, placing the killing in the early hours of the morning. He had been attacked with a heavy, blunt instrument, possibly a length of lead or steel pipe, according to Detective-Sergeant Framboise of the Homicide Squad, who viewed the body before it was removed from the scene of the crime.
>
> "'The killer,' Framboise said, 'approached Chesterley

from the front. This suggests that he may have been a friend of the victim. In any case, he used his weapon to crush the front of Chesterley's skull and mutilate the head but missed, broke the left collarbone and knocked the left shoulder from its socket in a downward dislocation. It seems clear that the crime was committed by a powerful man.'

"Police had no suggestions regarding the motive for the crime pending further investigation. Robbery apparently was not the motive, since Chesterley's wallet containing a large sum of money was found in his pocket.

"Chesterley, whose residence is a large home on McTavish Street, was a local citizen of considerable means whose occupation had not been ascertained up to press time. He was born in Montreal and, except for brief periods, had lived here his whole life.

"James Montgomery, who discovered the body, was taking an early morning stroll around the mountain when he noticed a dark form lying some distance from the side of the path he was climbing. Interviewed by reporters, he told the following story: 'At first, when I saw this figure, I thought it was some drunk sleeping off a hangover. I went on up the path. Then for some reason I looked back, and it seemed to me one arm of the form was bent at an unnatural angle.

"'I went back and as I approached I could see blood on the ground about the figure. He was lying on his face. When I turned him over I found just a lot of blood and pulp where his face should have been. I felt for his heartbeat, but of course he was cold and stiff. It seemed to me he had been dead for some time.'

"Montgomery, who is a research chemist employed

by the Associated Chemical Company, acted promptly and with great presence of mind. He ran down the mountain to the station maintained by the mountain police, and brought two constables back to the scene of the slaying. At the same time the officer in charge of the station relayed the news to headquarters, and a squad under Detective-Sergeant Framboise arrived in a short time. Montgomery did not allow the incident to interfere with his daily routine, and after returning to his apartment for breakfast went to his office, where he was interviewed by this reporter.

"This is the first murder to be committed this year in Mount Royal Park, the scene of brutal killings on many past occasions. It is unusual in the fact that robbery was not the overt cause of the crime, unless the criminal was disturbed before he could complete his gory task. Traditionally, mountain murders have been accompanied by robbery or in some instances moral offenses."

That was the newspaper story.

I read it in the course of a normal afternoon's work at the office. I wasn't working on a case, so I got the *Independent* at two p.m. and after I had worked through the various wars and revolutions on the first page, I got to this and read it.

So what, I thought.

Some wealthy citizen in a racket the boys would take a day or two to uncover had become a fifth wheel in his own machine. Then he'd been foolish enough to walk by himself on the mountain.

Framboise, who was an old friend of mine, was a man who jumped to as many conclusions as the laddy who hopped off the Jacques Cartier Bridge five times and was fished out each time. It didn't ring true, in my books, that someone just walked out of the dark and tapped Chesterley on the head. Not on Mount Royal after dark; nobody is that unsuspicious. I would have bet someone came up behind and held his arms while a second did the killing. And if the blows that missed Chesterley's head all landed on his left side, his attacker was a right-handed man.

There were enough right-handed men in the world that I didn't phone Framboise and tell him my brilliant deductions.

I sat with my feet on my desk and forgot the case while I read the comics. Dick Tracy was in bad trouble.

The phone rang. The voice of Allan MacArnold, reporter for the *Clarion*, came to me. MacArnold, boy alcoholic. He was a little bit lushed that early in the day; indefensible but not uncommon.

"Come join me," he said convivially.

"Why?" I asked coldly.

"Because I'm in the Trafalgar."

"And you want me to pick up your cheque?"

"No. I've got some interesting news."

"Tell me now."

"And the Trafalgar is a good place to drink. So you should come on over."

"All right," I said.

It would have been simpler, a lot less messy, and probably no more painful if I'd just pulled out my revolver and shot myself between the eyes right then, instead of leaving the office to meet MacArnold.

Chapter Two

I CAME OUT THE FRONT door of the Canam Building, which I theoretically inhabit from nine to five, and crossed Dominion Square, kicking the pigeons out of my way. Some people would say I was cruel, but at least I don't make friends with them so I can wring their necks and take them home for squab pie.

I was in no hurry to get to the Trafalgar so I crossed St. Catherine Street at Peel, walked up Peel three doorways, and immersed myself in the dank coolness of the Elephant Tavern. It was a sunny June day outside, warm for walking, and the beaded quart of Molson tasted like attar of ambrosia. I dawdled over it and looked around hoping a fight might develop in the place, but it was too early in the afternoon. I went out and walked on up Peel to Sherbrooke, and then west with the sun scorching my face until I came to the Trafalgar.

The Trafalgar. For me, it's as much a part of Montreal as the great electric cross atop Mount Royal. It's a little Sherbrooke Street hotel with a small, dark bar. All the waiters have worked in the bar at least fifteen years, and they all know me well enough to call me by name. Not that I'm a bar-snob, but it's nice to know that if you take one over the nine you'll be put to bed in a room upstairs, not in the gutter with a curbstone for a pillow.

I came to the Trafalgar and walked into the bar, and I was too late. There were three youngish women resting their feet after buying out Holt Renfrew, cooling their tongues with creme-de-menthe frappes. There were several parties of two or three men. There was one tired young business man, sitting alone, watching me as I came in. But there was no MacArnold.

Bob, the youngest and shortest of the waiters, padded up to me. "Afternoon, Mr. Teed," he said.

"I was supposed to meet Allan MacArnold here," I told him.

Bob started to say, "Mr. MacArnold is—". But the tired young man had hoisted himself to his feet, and interrupted.

"MacArnold's over here," he said. "He got a little tired and he's resting. I'm Jimmy Montgomery. We were waiting for you."

A tired young business man, I'd called him. He was slim, wiry, three inches shorter than my own six feet, and I'd say about 35 years old. His hair was wiry as he was, strong sandy hair that oscillated back over his skull in a series of perfectly uniform waves. But I don't mean he was a pretty boy. He had a lean and spare face with a strong jutting jaw and narrow, straight nose. His pale blue eyes were wideset under light brows, and his skin was mottled with freckles. He had a small white scar in his upper lip and another above one eye, not disfiguring marks but enough to suggest he might be a very competent bar room fighter if aroused.

I guess I stared at him a little too long, because he grinned a rather sheepish grin and said, "Yeah, that's right. I'm *that* Jimmy Montgomery."

"What Jimmy Montgomery?"

"I found a body on top of Mount Royal this morning. I thought maybe you'd read it in the papers."

"Oh, sure," I grinned back. "I remember. What I liked best was it didn't spoil your breakfast."

"The hell it didn't."

"That's what the paper said."

"Reporters have to say something." He shrugged. "Like that story about me taking a walk on the mountain every morning. Hell, I'd been out on an all-night toot and walked home across the mountain to sober up. I didn't want them to print that, so I told them to use their imagination."

"I think I'm going to like you," I said candidly. "Tell me, where's MacArnold?"

Montgomery pointed. There was a semi-circular sofa beside the chair he'd been sitting in. It was a substantial, high-backed affair and I had to walk right up to it to see that there was anyone in it.

In the semi-circular sofa was a semi-circular MacArnold. He was laid out neatly, following the contour of the furniture, like a tired sickle lying on a shelf. He was snoring.

MacArnold, the prize of the morning *Clarion*, was a man who always wore a tweed jacket which never matched the tweed pants he always wore. He claimed it was impossible to keep a press in these tweeds, and his appearance gave no reason to doubt his word. MacArnold was a black Scotsman, with skin so thick and heavily pigmented doctors always thought him anaemic and jet hair, smooth and a bit thin on his wide skull. He had heavy lips that might be called sensuous unless you knew the thing they most loved to touch was the rim of a glass.

I shook his bony shoulder. "Hey, wake up!"

No response. Bob, the waiter, was circling around with an expression half between amusement and disapproval. "Get me a tall glass of ice water, Bob," I said grimly.

MacArnold opened one eye wide. "No, you don't," he muttered. He dropped his lank legs to the floor and stretched his convex spinal column back to concave. He looked at me balefully. He said, "And I asked you here to do you a favor."

"And I'm doing you a favor," I pointed out. "I'm getting

worried about you. I think I'll read you the lesson right now."

Montgomery was either a sensitive type, or he felt a bit responsible for getting MacArnold drunk so early in the day. He colored slightly and edged off on a stroll that took him to the men's room.

"Look," I told MacArnold, "I love you like a brother."

"As well as anyone but yourself, I'm sure."

"—And therefore, you by-line bum, from now on I'm going to beat you up every time I find you like this. I've seen too many newsguys go this way. You get off work at a morning paper in the small hours, and you want a little fun, so you have some short snorts. That takes till around breakfast time. Okay, if you go home and get some sleep then, and wake up and live a healthy afternoon. But once you start hitting it right through the day, too, you're on the road the pink and purple snakes travel to meet you. I know. I worked on the *Clarion* once, too, remember?"

"Yeah. But listen," he said defensively, "you know I don't make this a habit. As it happens, I'm still on an assignment—that guy Montgomery."

"That was killed in the afternoon papers," I said, "and you know it, and I know it, and your City Editor Hatch knows it, unless he's losing his touch."

"Not the point. It broke away too late for today's *Clarion*, of course. But for tomorrow, we've got eight more hours from now to get some idea of why this guy Chesterley was killed—which is probably tied up with whatever racket he was in—or perhaps even start solving the crime."

"Ha," I said. "Ha, ha."

"Some killing get solved that fast."

"Tell me. Is this the big favour you're doing me? Are you dragging me in to help you solve this crime, and if so, who's paying me?"

"Nobody. If you have any free ideas you want to hand out, of course, that's fine. But I'm not too interested because I've got my own ideas on this one. What I called you in here for is something entirely different."

"Well, tell me that, if you can grope through the whiskey mist in your head and remember."

"Crawfie Foster is back in town."

"My, my," I said, only because the other things I thought of saying would get me thrown out of the Trafalgar. "Well, I don't know what I can do about it. And I'm sure not scared of anything he might do to me."

"He got five years after you fingered him for a doper. But apparently he was a good boy in the pen; he got paroled."

Crawfie Foster was a weak-eyed, weak-kneed, weak-charactered little photographer who had weaseled his way into a dope ring in Montreal. I'd stumbled on the ring while trying to clean up a double murder, and in the chaos that followed most of its members got killed. Crawfie had come out of it with only a flesh wound, which was too bad—and I suppose that's the first time I've said that about anyone. It shows what I thought of Crawfie Foster.

We dropped the topic, because just then Jimmy Montgomery came back. He was a man who got thirsty quickly. He'd only been away from his drink five minutes, but he put way one entire pint of Molson in about two swigs before he settled back to calm guzzling.

"Not that I'm interested in this thing," I said, "but what is it Mr. Montgomery knows that's going to give you a new lead in this murder on the mountain?"

"I don't know," Montgomery said frankly.

"I'm just stumbling along," MacArnold said.

I signalled Bob and got more Molson all around. I figured there was enough conversation to last one more pint. "You don't solve murders, just stumbling along," I commented.

"I beg your pardon?" MacArnold said with a heavy sarcasm. I ignored that. "It's the way *you* solve them," he went on, determined to get a rise.

Montgomery said, "From what I've read, he sure muddled through to a solution a few times."

"Over a pile of corpses," MacArnold grunted.

"I don't muddle," I said with dignity. "I follow leads."

"I'm following leads," said the *Clarion*'s oracle.

"Such as?"

MacArnold shot a glance at Jimmy Montgomery. For some reason, he obviously didn't want to say much with the chemist listening. After a pause he said briefly, "Gambling. Chesterley was a gambler, I'm told. That's what the afternoon papers missed."

"I thought it might be something like that."

Montgomery broke in. "I didn't know that. I didn't know anything about Chesterley. That's why I can't see what use I'll be to you, MacArnold. All I know is what I saw."

"Stick around," MacArnold told him. "You don't know what you saw. At least, things you saw that don't mean anything now may fit into a picture, later on."

"But I didn't see anything that—"

"Do like MacArnold says," I advised him. "Stick around. Maybe you'll suddenly remember he wore a shirt that could be bought only in Cincinnati. That ties him in with a Cincinnati gambling mob who moved to Montreal to operate, MacArnold draws his pencil and rounds up the rest of the gang, and the case is solved."

"Sure, be bright," MacArnold said bitterly. "Just the same, something like that could happen."

"Absolutely. Stick around," I advised Montgomery again.

"Stick around just as long as MacArnold is buying the beer."

I sold that one for my exit line and got up and away from the table before MacArnold tried to buy more insults. But I only went as far as the door. There, just as I tried to get out, a suave-looking couple appeared, blocking my way.

The man I'd known years before, when we went to McGill together. His name was Paul Hanwood, he'd taken Commerce and then graduated into his family firm—which was a good one—and he was tall and nicely-groomed and well-dressed and I didn't waste any more time even thinking about him. I couldn't even see him for the tower of elegance that leaned on his arm.

She was the kind of girl who dressed to seem svelte and slender as a *Vogue* model, and yet all those curves that make a woman a woman whispered at your blood until it almost sizzled. She was dark, but I couldn't even tell you what color her eyes were—the general impression was what was lifting me off the floor. She had clothes so perfect they must have been pressed after she put them on and a skin fresher than warm milk foaming in a pail. She was a tall girl, with a surface coolness that made you feel you should approach her with a gift, begging acceptance. And there was an underlying warmth that would make it worthwhile.

Paul Hanwood spoke to me. A good thing; it would have been very embarrassing to speak to him and find he didn't remember me.

"Hello, Russ."

"How are you, Paul?"

"Don't I see the demon reporter MacArnold in the corner? What are you two dreaming up now—another string of murders?"

"No. We were drawn here by mutual thirst."

Hanwood turned to the girl. "This is Russell Teed, darling. He's Montreal's version of the tough private eye—you know, you've met them in American movies."

She smiled. Her teeth were a delicate, soft white and uneven enough to have some character. The smile did things to her eyes. "You do not have a battered enough face to be typical, Mr. Teed," she said.

I gulped. "I have all kinds of scars, but I try to keep them hidden in public," I said, "Miss—"

"Elena Giotto," Hanwood filled in, almost purring the soft Italian name.

"People have been very considerate, Miss Giotto. I seem to get shot mostly in the extremities."

Paul Hanwood snapped his fingers. "I have it! There was a dead man lying on top of Mount Royal this morning. I suppose you're going to work up a few more murders from that."

"Not if I can help it. And anyway, you're wrong. I'm just not concerned in the case."

"Oh," he said disappointed. "I was looking forward to a few interesting by-line stories from MacArnold. A little gore with my breakfast marmalade and coffee. Too bad. See that you get into something soon."

"Definitely."

"Be seeing you." He smiled, grasped Elena firmly by the elbow, and pushed off for a table. I tried to think of a quick excuse to join them, but I'd clearly been on my way out when we met and I didn't want to be too obvious. Paul was much too attached to Elena. It would have to wait.

I got halfway through the door before a loud and clear Bronx cheer hit my ears. I turned around. MacArnold had his face buried in a beer glass and was studiously looking in another direction.

I came back, grasped the beer glass with a firm hand

and raised it until the beer began running out of his nose. He spluttered. He began to laugh. "Little gentleman," he scoffed. "'People have been very considerate, Miss Giotto,'" he mimicked. "Who you trying to impress, you run-down peeper?"

"Not you."

"Good, because you don't."

"Why don't you go solve your crime and leave me out of it? Sometimes I wish I'd never met you. I'm beginning to get dragged down to your level."

I sat down at the table, mainly because my empty glass hadn't been removed and there was still a pint of someone's beer to pour in it. "You see," I explained to Montgomery, "I used to be a respectable, refined private investigator—not too many years ago. I worked on clean, bloodless cases like embezzlement and grand larceny and stock swindles. Not a drop of gore ever soiled my hands. Then I met MacArnold, and I started meeting corpses at the same time. I don't say he brought them into my life, but somehow in my mind they're associated with him. Now what happens? Anybody in Montreal has a nice, private murder on their hands that they don't want to bother the police with, they call Teed. But do businessmen come to me any more to find out which Mexican hamlet the Comptroller went to, after he auctioned off the company's Alberta oil leases? They do not. I have no peace. I get little sleep. All the girls I meet would shoot grandmother for a few little emeralds and rubies. It's hell."

"It's your own fault," MacArnold pointed out.

"Maybe, but I blame you as much as I can. And this time, drag the bait in front of my nose as long as you want to. I won't bite any faster than a cob would rise to a dry fly. You want me in this case, don't you?"

"I didn't say so."

"You didn't have to," I told him, with my usual brilliant perception. "And if you did, it wouldn't work. So long. See you at A.A."

Montgomery was laughing into his beer.

Teed was walking out of the Trafalgar bar. And this time, I really got out.

I walked from Sherbrooke Street back down toward St. Catherine, heading for the garage near Dominion Square where I kept my Riley roadster parked in business hours.

It was a three-block walk, and on the way I got thirsty again. I almost got past the door of the Elephant Tavern, but not quite.

I went in there to drink, not to think things over. But to tell the truth, I was spoiling for something to think about. I hadn't had a case for a month, everybody interesting was out of town for the season, and the stock market was so dead you couldn't even play with mining securities.

I thought about the body on top of Mount Royal, and decided there was either nothing much in it that wouldn't be solved by a few days of routine police work, or there was nothing in it at all except attempted robbery, in which case it might never be solved. But that made very little of a mystery to it.

I thought about Montgomery, and decided he was probably just what he seemed, a normal young business guy who enjoyed his beer and his nights on the town, and I thought MacArnold was playing an outside chance if he expected to get anything from him.

Then I thought about Crawfie Foster. That was a different kettle of herring altogether and aroused more enthusiasm. If I continued idle for a while longer, I was going to do a little work on Crawfie and find out what he was doing back in Montreal. If it was crooked—and I couldn't imagine the guy doing anything straight—I'd make it my business to have him copped, just for the satisfaction it would give me.

Finally I thought about Elena Giotto. And I decided that was the most urgent project before the committee of one, and I'd better start right in on a campaign map.

Chapter Three

SOMEHOW THE THINKING-DRINKING session at the Elephant lasted longer than I expected or realized. By the time I stumbled to my feet it was almost dark and all the beer in me was brimming my stomach, giving me a heavy full feeling and cooling the cockles of my heart, which the alcohol had briefly warmed.

This type of afternoon is an occupational hazard of a private investigator between jobs.

I decided my car could sit in its downtown garage for the night; I would walk home and restore my vitality. I poked along St. Catherine Street from Peel to Guy, window shopping and pausing to get makings for dinner. Then I started the long climb up Guy and Cote des Neiges to my home, my apartment in the big square building just opposite the beginning of Westmount Boulevard. It was cool, and a little breeze rustled the leaves as I walked. There were trees almost all the way; Montreal is a good city for trees.

When I came into the apartment I locked the door carefully again behind me. I still thought MacArnold might barge back into my ken at any minute to get me tangled up with his mountain body, and that was something to be avoided.

I felt so fine after the long walk that I automatically uncapped a pint of Dow as I walked into the kitchen. The very sight of the beer reminded me I had urgent business to transact in another room. When I got back from the bathroom, I recapped the bottle and got out the Scotch bottle instead. A man's effluent system can stand just so much.

With the Scotch for inspiration, I settled down to work. I assembled a quart of bulk oysters, a can of cream of mushroom soup, a cupful of bread crumbs and a few appropriate seasonings including sherry. The oysters got cooked on top of the stove in their own juice until they curled at the edges, while the undiluted soup was thickening up a bit more in the double boiler. The bread crumbs I mixed up with a generous dollop of butter. Then everything went into a casserole dish and into the broiler for ten minutes to brown the crumbs and warm up the sherry, and when it came out it smelled so good I just ate it right there in the kitchen, out of the casserole.

I brewed coffee, unwrapped a wedge of camembert, and carted a tray into my living room. I poured a few liquid gold drops of cognac into a snifter to go with the coffee, and I took my shoes off so I could put my feet up on my chesterfield, and then I relaxed in perfect contentment.

So the door buzzer burped.

I went to the door with my shoes off, my jacket off and my tie under my left ear. Anyone who interrupted me just then could take me as he found me. I opened the door. Then, without even thinking about it, I straightened my tie.

"Elena!" I said joyfully. Then I collected myself and decided if she was chasing, I was running. I carefully put my tie back where it was before and said, but casually, "Don't you think you're rushing things a bit?"

"I beg your pardon?" The tall and slim brunette was very distant in her surface coolness. She even retreated one step. For a minute I was afraid I might have to run after her in my stocking feet to bring her in.

"Well, well, come in," I said. "We were just going to have coffee. You and I. Come in."

She stepped hesitantly across the threshold and I waited

to snap the door shut behind her as soon as she was out of the angle of slam.

"I was looking for a Mr. George Potts," she said firmly.

"I'm Russell Teed. Remember?"

"And my name," she said, "is not Elena. It isn't anything like Elena."

"Elena is what Paul Hanwood called you, and Elena is good enough for me."

She eyed me with a mounting degree of suspicion. "What are we playing—anagrams? Hanwood, Schmanwood! Does George Potts live here? If not, which is his apartment?"

"Potts, pans," I said. "I've lived here eight years and the only Potts in the neighborhood are the ones that get thrown at cat-fights after dark." I got a little impatient. "Come in so I can close the door. We can argue inside."

She shrugged. She came in from the rather dim corridor, and after I closed the door she followed me through the entry and into the relative brightness of my living room.

She stood rigidly then just beyond the edge of my thick, dark green rug. The rug's shaggy pile grew up over the toeless tips of her little shoes, and took a bit of height away from the spike heels. She had very sheer, dark stockings like a delicate layer of smoke over her slim legs. She wore a dress of heavy moire silk cut in striking, almost swashbuckling lines—no doubt an original by somebody. It was dark green, not a matching color to my rug, but not one that fought. That was good because I figured to keep her in the room as long as I could.

She had the cool face and hot eyes that belonged to Elena Giotto; a slim face with hollowed cheeks and piquant, almost exotic angles to the bone structure. The face framed her eyes and set them off, giving them a depth and expression more like a fine painting than a living room. I had a notion you could look into those eyes and believe her either an angel or a red, sizzling little devil.

I looked at her for a while, and as I looked my face slowly got longer and longer, like a kid's when you tell him the bananas in the centrepiece are just wax.

The corners of my mouth turned down. "Oh, oh," I said.

"Well?"

"I take it all back. I apologize. I'll even try to find George Potts for you."

"You're willing to admit you made a mistake? Maybe it wasn't a line, then," she guessed. "Or maybe it was, and this is still part of it. Well, I'm in here now."

I came to with a start. "You sure are. Pardon me. I'll get you a cup. Sit down." I started for the kitchen. I looked back over my shoulder. "Maybe you think it's impossible. I'm inclined to think so myself. How could I meet two brunettes that look as much alike as you and Elena Giotto, in the same day?"

It was a rhetorical question. She didn't try to answer it. When I came back and poured her coffee she asked, "Who is Elena Giotto?"

"The hell with Elena," I told her. "Who are you?"

"Call me Lila."

"Lila who? I told you my last name."

"I've forgotten it."

"Teed. Russell Teed."

"Oh. The private detective."

"A private detective."

She looked around the room, at the yellow walls and the brown walls and the dark green rug; at the light-yellow brick fireplace and the lemon-background patterned upholstery on the chesterfield suite, and all the built-in brown and yellow shelves around the walls where my books and magazines and records were.

"I'd say you did pretty well for yourself," she commented.

"As well as I can. I don't work for charity. Somebody was trying to rouse my demon curiosity this afternoon, to get some free work out of me. I made it very clear to them."

"Oh?" She sounded quite interested.

"Let's skip the shop talk. Tell me who you are."

"I'm the girl who was looking for George Potts, remember? I'm still looking for him."

"Why bother?"

"It's business, Mr. Teed. I happen to be a public steno." She reached into the leather map-case she trucked around for a handbag and flourished a dictation notebook. "I got a call to come around and take some letters for Mr. George Potts, this address. His name wasn't on a mailbox downstairs so I came up to look around, and punched your buzzer to ask directions."

"No George Potts," I said. "You could try asking the janitor."

"He didn't answer his bell. This is a heck of a note, at this time of day."

"Do you often go out on night calls?"

"I do."

"Little dangerous, isn't it, for a girl as beautiful as you are?"

"Why, Mr. Teed!" she said, with corny coyness.

I noticed she was letting her coffee sit there and get cold. I pulled out a deck of State Express and fed her one and lit hers and mine. I indicated the coffee. "Maybe you'd sooner have a drink. Scotch, rye?"

"Since I'm here, thanks. Scotch. May I come with you and inspect the other parts of this establishment?"

"Sure."

I led the way out of the living room, into the entry, and along the corridor to the kitchen. She stopped to examine something in the neighborhood of the front door, and then arrived in the kitchen.

I was a little embarrassed by the seven or eight empty beer quarts spaced around the kitchen, and the dinner dishes I hadn't cleared up yet. I commenced the conversation on other lines. "Funny, my mistaking you for Elena Giotto," I said. "The face isn't really much the same. Just the coloring and the black hair. And the figure. Of course, the figure. You both have the same type of figure. Excellent, if I may be so personal. But a little unbelievable."

"It's my figure," she said aroused. "I don't know anything about this Elena Gee-otto, but I resent it if somebody doesn't believe in mine. What's wrong with it?"

I looked her over very carefully. She watched me with a this-had-better-be-good expression.

"The falsies," I said, "are just plain too large for the rest of chassis. It's nice, but it's unbelievable."

"The *what*?" she screamed.

"Falsies," I said apologetically. "After all, you asked me."

She was trying to make up her mind whether or not to hit me. She decided not to. She'd thought of something better to do.

The dress opened very easily. Buttons down its front weren't fake; they actually opened up. Maybe she had a petticoat on, but she wasn't wearing any slip. She threw the unbuttoned dress back off her shoulders and exposed the laciest black brassiere I ever saw. Practically pure lace.

"Well?"

I looked. I enjoyed looking. "Okay, no foam rubber," I said.

There was a nasty whistling sound just above my left ear that gave me warning I'd been suckered. I had time to move my head about an inch on my shoulders before the sap came down. Instead of landing solidly behind my ear it grazed my head and bounced fairly harmlessly off the back of my shoulder.

A sap, the popular weapon of silent attack, is the same general idea as an old sock filled with sand. Only in the case of a sap you have a little leather pouch, with long thongs for swinging, usually loaded with lead shot. Swung with a good follow-through, it picks up a hell of a lot of momentum before it sinks into a tender part of the skull.

I'd been pouring the drinks while Lila and I talked and I still had my hand wrapped around the bottle. I swung with it, pivoting around and aiming for the spot where the sapper's head should have been. For a completely blind shot, it wasn't too bad. I almost got him, but he saw the bottle coming and threw himself right backwards onto the floor. The bottle went over his head an inch high and leaving my hand, hit the wall with a glorious smash. The place immediately began to smell like a lost week-end.

I started to throw myself on the prone crook when I saw the second one. He was coming at me slowly with a gun held very high. He wasn't going to shoot. He was looking for something to hit, and not a fly on the table either.

The floored thug just lay there with his knees drawn up and his feet pointed toward me, protecting most of his vital areas. He watched me sharply out of a pair of the baggiest eyes this side of the monkey house. He was scrawny, with skin as dark and wrinkled as the leather of a soft, old boot. The mug with the gun was the muscles of the team. He looked about six foot six and his shoulders would touch both sides of the average doorway. He wasn't too well shaved and his face looked more like the back end of a steel-grey bus than like ordinary flesh. He had large eyes, a peculiar pale brown color, about as full of expression as a parson's curse.

I had two kitchen chairs and a table, all within reach and not bolted to the floor, to work with. I got one chair by the back and charged the gorilla with it. He stepped back and the only damage I did was to knock his gun out of his hand. As I lunged past the scrawny one, he lashed out and got me with both heels on my right kneecap. That put the leg out of commission and I had to hop. Up until then I'd figured on dodging past them to the hallway and getting my revolver out of the holster in the hall closet; maybe they were afraid to shoot, but I wasn't.

Now that was out. I pivoted to the right on my one good leg and broke the kitchen chair carefully over the leathery little lug's sad face. Part of the seat disappeared into his cheek and one of the legs broke so the splintered end tore away a good chunk of his ear. He screamed like a wet baby but didn't go out. I had to jump on his stomach which was tricky with one bad leg, but I hit the right spot and he went flat as a cheap football after a rough scrimmage.

Muscles was still scrambling in the corner for his gun.

I stole a look over my shoulder to make sure Lila wasn't creeping up on me. She wasn't, but she had ideas. She'd found it easier to step out of the dress than to try climbing back into it. I was wrong about the petticoat; all she had on now was the brassiere and a matching pair of black panties that were just as lacy and far more revealing. She was beautifully constructed, but that wasn't half as important as the fact that she was waiting, poised, with one of the empty beer bottles in her hand. She was getting in position to brain somebody, and I didn't think for a moment her sympathies were with me.

I picked up the second kitchen chair and let it go at her. I didn't even watch it land, but took off from my one leg and landed on Muscle's back. I chopped him twice behind the ear with the edge of my hand and he sagged slightly and shook his head like a spaniel getting water out of its ears.

Just then there was a crunch and a splintering crash, and a big black cloud swelled up behind my eyes and began blacking out the whole scene.

Lila? I thought. Short for Delilah, that was.

Chapter Four

I came to with the front door buzzing. And that wasn't all. The door would buzz for a minute, and then my head would buzz right back. They were having a little contest and I think my head was winning. It was buzzing a lot louder.

It was daylight. It was morning. Maybe it was afternoon. How was I to know? All I knew was my face was down in the hard blue linoleum of my kitchen floor. My nose was a little flat and tired from being slept on. Around my head, as I lifted it a few inches, was a wide green halo of broken beer bottle glass. I wished I'd been more faithful in my prayers to the patron saint of bar-room brawlers.

I moved my eyes a little to the left and the right. They moved in creaky jerks, like an outdoor gate in the wintertime. Over to the right I saw a quantity of dried blood on the floor where I'd slugged leather-face with the chair, and that made me happy. I noticed another pool of blood, nearer me and bigger, and got unhappy again. It struck me the bigger pool was probably my own blood.

I had a problem on my mind. To some people it might look like a skull, but to me it was just a problem. I got my hand up to the back of my head and felt soft and spongy. The hair was matted and caked with blood. I pulled two small chunks of glass out of the matted hair, and it was like pulling teeth with your bare hands and no novocaine.

The door buzzer kept on nattering. So did my head. I made the supreme effort and crawled to a sitting position. To make things complete, I sat on a sharp piece of broken glass.

I pulled up my trouser leg to look at my ruined knee; that is, I tried. The knee was so swollen I couldn't get the cloth rolled up over it. I gave up, got my sound leg under me, and stood.

The door buzzed. Maybe you will forgive me. I lost my temper. I picked an empty beer quart off the table and whaled it at the buzzer, high on the wall. I hit it first time, and it didn't buzz any more after that.

I hopped two hops to the sink. I had a vegetable spray attachment on the tap, and I shot cold water through it and ducked underneath. Blood roared to my head but then the cold water began to bite into the spongy patch of skull. It smarted like iodine, but I began to come around. Little bits of dried blood slowly detached themselves from me and built up in the drain filter.

I turned off the cold water and shoved myself upright. Then I heard my front door opening. There was one hesitant step in my entry. I picked up another empty beer quart and hobbled to the corridor. It was costing me five cents for every bottle that got broken, but I was willing to sacrifice another.

There was a girl standing beside my open front door.

She was petite and not aggressively female of figure. She was wearing a simple light frock that gave her a little-girl look, and she was glancing around as though she wondered whether she should have stepped in and was about eighty per cent sure she shouldn't.

"My God!" I said in brittle tones. "Another brunette!"

She jumped about six inches at the sound of my voice. She turned and saw me, and then she did more than jump. She put her fist up to her mouth and almost swallowed it keeping back her scream.

I hadn't looked in a mirror yet, but I could imagine what she was screaming at.

"Shut the door behind you, and come in," I said crossly.

It didn't sound like my voice. It sounded very far away and full of gravel. Only the crossness sounded like what I'd meant.

"Look," I said as the kid continued to stand there, "you don't have to be scared. It's only old Teed recovering from an all night binge. I'm quite sober now, thank you. And I seem to have hit myself on the back of the head, where I can't reach to put a bandage on."

She stood. "So come in!" I yelled, so loud she jumped again. "I don't care who you are or why you came here. I just want help. You can at least make coffee, can't you?"

Tears started in her eyes and she bobbed her head gravely, yes, like a little school girl getting hell from the head mistress. She took her fist out of her mouth. "Mr.—Teed?" she gulped.

"I wish it were Harry Truman," I assured her.

"Mr. MacArnold of the *Clarion* sent me here to see you because I was working for Mr. Foster and he won't pay me and I can't find him and Mr. MacArnold thought you might help me because he said you knew Mr. Foster and might have an interest in finding him and getting me—" At that point she had used up all her small lung capacity and her voice ran down.

"Sure, sure," I said. "I'll do anything for you, after I pick up all the little pieces of my skull from the floor and fit them back into my head. Come on out here and help."

She followed me meekly back into the kitchen.

"My!" she said. "Did you have a party?"

It seemed awfully close to a crack, but you couldn't mistake the innocence in her voice. What a kid to be mixed up with Crawfie Foster!

"I was suckered," I said. "Without going into too many details, the story is that a woman came in here on a pretext. When I wasn't watching she slipped the latch off the front door. Then she came out here and talked to me while two bozos sneaked up on me from behind." I looked at the shambles. There was broken glass all over the floor, along with blood; the furniture was all shoved crooked, one kitchen chair was smashed and the other lay on its side in the corner. "I am happy to say I put up a fight."

I hobbled to the unbroken chair, righted it and sat down heavily. "Does the sight of open wounds bother you?" I asked.

The kid came into her own. She walked around behind me and looked at the back of my skull. "I've seen worse than that when a skier hit a tree," she said calmly. "I'm a Ski Patroller, and I know first aid. I've also had to use it before, so don't think I'll just make things worse. None of my patients has ever died."

"What you need is a basin—look under the sink. Sterile gauze, a big role of it, in the bathroom cupboard—out and down the corridor to your left. And there's some fairly pure soap in the bathroom, too."

She assembled the material, drew a basinful of hot water, and went quietly to work. Her efficiency extended to putting a pit of coffee on the stove at the same time. I lit cigarettes one after the other and let her clean up the damage. After she got most of the corruption out of the way she studies the gashes in my scalp and said, "You're all right. You haven't got a skull fracture, or you'd have concussion. You could have the concussion, of course, without a fracture, but you wouldn't be as operational as this with any concussion."

"If I had concussion, I slept it off," I said. "What time is it?"

"About ten o'clock."

She put a thick gauze pad over the wounds and covered

my head with a skull cap anchored by adhesive tape. I picked up a shiny frying pan and studied myself in it. "Doctor Brent," I said, "call surgery. All I need is a nose mask."

It wasn't too good, but she giggled. Then she poured the coffee. I drank three cups black and felt nearly human. I was getting low in cigarettes, but that was all right because she didn't smoke.

"Well, my friend and benefactor," I finally said, "tell me your story now. Who are you?"

"Priscilla Dover."

"They call you Pris?"

"No," she said solemnly. "Priscilla."

"How in the name of the Sistine Madonna did you manage to get mixed up with Foster?"

"Photography is my hobby," she said. "I do a lot of skiing in the wintertime, and hiking around the Laurentians in the other seasons, and take landscapes with my camera. It's a Voigtlander reflex with an f3.5 Voigtar lens."

"I don't know an f3.5 lens from the Palomar telescope," I said, "but go on."

"About a month ago this classified ad appeared in the *Clarion*, for girls who could take photographs to work as picture-takers in night clubs. I was looking for a job at the time and I thought it might be fun. Besides, the ad said the pay was good," she told me ruefully. "The promised pay was good all right, but I never was able to collect."

"So you answered this ad, and met Crawfie Foster?"

"That's right. He gave me the job, and a Speed Graphic. I had three night clubs to cover each evening."

"What did you think of Foster when you met him?"

"Oh—I don't suppose I liked him very much. Remember, I was trying to get this job from him, so I was trying to impress him. I paid more attention to my attitude than to his. But he didn't strike me as anyone who would be troublesome. Not a—" she hesitated and stammered a little, "—a wolf, or anything."

"No, his weakness isn't sex," I admitted.

"He seemed to know his business. He was going to run the dark room and develop the pictures. He had a pretty nice set-up for turning out prints rapidly—you know, automatic drum drier and so on. Three of us were working for him."

"If there were three of you, each covering three clubs, you had a lot of the business in town sewed up," I mused. "There have been people with those concessions for years. I wonder how Crawfie wormed in and took over."

"He said something about that. Said he was paying a higher price than anyone for the concessions, and he could afford to pay us well too and still stay in business because he was turning out a superior product and could charge the customers a higher price."

"Was there any truth in that?"

"Yes. We had coupled range finders on the cameras and we had to be very careful to get good focus—sharp negatives. Then Foster blew them up to about twice the size of usual night club snaps. There's very little extra cost in doing that—just the increased amount of paper you use. But the pics look a lot more expensive, so we charged plenty for them."

"All sounds fairly reasonable," I admitted. "If I didn't know Crawfie so well, I'd think it was on the up-and-up."

"This is what happened," she went on, and her voice was very angry. "We were to be paid at the end of the month. Of course, we got some tips, but they didn't amount to a great deal. Crawfie had promised us two hundred each for the month—good pay. Well, I guess he expected to make it a profitable business by welching on us. The end of the month, when we showed up in the early evening to get our cameras and go to work—and incidentally to get paid—the studio was locked."

"Where was the place?"

"On Peel above St. Catherine—the other side of the street from the Mount Royal Hotel." She gave me the number. "It was a small office building, with a tavern on the ground floor."

"The Elephant Tavern."

"That's right. Well, the three of us waited around, thinking Foster was late. That had happened before. After an hour, though, one of the girls went for the janitor. She thought we might at least get our cameras, so we could start work. The janitor said Foster had moved out of the studio, with all his equipment, that afternoon. He had a month-to-month lease on the space, and he'd given it up after just the one month."

"He'd have to give a month's notice," I said, "or pay the second month's rent. I can't imagine him doing that, so I would guess he only took the place for a month in the first instance."

"It fits in with my idea," she said. "That means he expected all along to skip out at the end of the month, with his bills and our wages unpaid. That way he probably ran the business for the whole month with the studio rent his only cost. Everything else would be pure profit, and believe me, there is money in the night club picture business. One night I brought in three hundred dollars, and it was seldom under a hundred."

I thought it over a little bit. I went absently over to the fridge and pulled out a pint of Dow. I waved it at Priscilla. "Have one?"

"No thanks. I don't drink."

"Don't drink beer? How about a rye and ginger, or—"

"I just don't drink, thanks."

"Well, a Coke?"

"I've had coffee," she said. "That's my caffeine for this morning. I'll settle for a ginger ale."

I poured one for her, silently. It all sounded a little old-maidish, but somehow her attitude suited her. It went with that wholesome, little girl appearance. And it also impressed me that however she felt, she gave no faint signs of disapproval as I poured myself the beer.

I drank half the beer and went through a State Express, still trying to think the business through. Finally I frowned and shook my head. "It doesn't add up at all. If he went to all that trouble to set the business up, it wasn't a one-month proposition. Something happened to make him skip. And of course, being Crawfie, he skipped without paying anyone off."

"Perhaps he thought he could work the racket over and over again, moving every month."

"Not in Montreal, he couldn't. And it would hardly pay to try the stunt each month in a different city."

"Well—whatever happened, I'd like my two hundred dollars. I could use it. But I don't suppose I'll ever see it."

"How much looking for him have you done?"

"The other two girls and I reported the whole business to the police. They checked. Foster had been living in a cheap hotel on Windsor Street; he checked out of there, leaving no forwarding address, of course. He had settled with the landlord of his business block and left no address there. And no one has been located who remembers the truck that moved him away. The police put out a routine check to all registered trucking companies, asking if they'd moved him, and if so, to what address, but they aren't too hopeful. They think he probably picked up a couple of men, with a truck, casually, to avoid being traced."

"Doesn't sound too promising. We don't even know whether he moved to another place in town, or right out of the city."

"No. No one had seen him since the end of the month."

"It's possible, if he weren't going to start a business again right away, that he'd have his equipment stored."

"The police are checking storage companies, too."

I shrugged.

"Will you be able to help me? I don't imagine I could pay your usual fees, but we three girls would chip in—"

"Skip it," I said. "I'll help you, all right. For free—if you won't tell the detective's union. Not because I love you but because I hate Crawfie."

"Why?"

"You want the story? A few years ago, a little Montreal druggist named Herbinger was a go-between in a big drug racket here in Montreal. He received dope off ships that berthed here from Europe, and passed it on to another party who smuggled it into the United States. How I tangled with them is part of another story—the hide-out where the dope was transferred from Herbinger to the smuggler was the scene of another crime. But anyhow, Crawfie Foster was a friend of Herbinger's. He stumbled onto the fact that Herbinger was dealing in dope, and demanded to be cut in. They gave him the local business—he got a supply from the druggist and peddled it around the city. I fixed him by telling the Mounties the whole set-up, and Crawfie landed in a federal pen. He didn't stay there half as long as he should have. I'm naturally interested in what he's doing now that he's out."

"I see. But why should you hate him?"

"You wouldn't know anything about dope," I said, "but if you ever saw what it did to people, you'd hate dope-sellers the way you hate cockroaches in your kitchen. And Crawfie actually introduced people to the stuff—made addicts out of them. At the end of this old case Herbinger committed suicide and most of the other dopers got shot. Crawfie is the only one loose. I'm checking on him, as long as he's around—to make sure he never sells dope again, first of all. And if he does anything else that could put him back behind bars, I'll be happy to help him there."

I'd done too much talking, or maybe it was the pint of beer. My head was trying to crack itself open from the inside. There was a pain that started right behind my eyes and shot back through my skull like a shell fired from a naval gun, hit the soft spot on my skull and tried to burst right through. They came about every five seconds, and in a minute or two one would burst out and ricochet around the room.

I got to my feet weakly, and my bad leg tried to buckle under me. I shifted all my weight to the good one.

"I don't feel so well," I told Priscilla. "I'm going to lie down a while. Call me some time tomorrow, and maybe I'll have an angle. I'll work on it."

She looked at me sympathetically. "Can I stay and help?"

"Nope. Just got a cracking headache, for obvious reasons. I'll take some stuff and lie down."

I limped to the front door with her. I locked it after she left, and put on the night lock, and secured the safety chain. Enough of this nonsense. If the building caught on fire they'd have to uses axes to get me out.

I limped to the bathroom and fished in the cupboard. I found a little vial and took two Frosst 292s, with about a grain of codeine in them. I washed them down with the last of the beer and went in and sprawled on my bed. After a while the headache dulled, and I went to sleep.

I woke later, with the sun still high. It was early afternoon. I crawled into a shower and stayed there for some time, and when I got out I felt almost able to eat. It was the first intimation I'd had that my system was back to running on anything but codeine and ethyl alcohol.

I tested the bad knee. I felt it and as far as I could tell through the swelling, there was nothing seriously broken. I put a little weight on it. I got the roll of one-inch adhesive and taped it up tighter than a fat girl's best shoes. I couldn't bend the knee, and that gave me quite a limp, but I could walk.

Then I heard a heavy pounding on my door—a metallic clanking, as though someone was beating it with an old tire iron. Ah, yes. I'd broken the buzzer. Whoever was there had likely been buzzing for a long time and decided only noise would waken me.

I draped myself in a four-foot towel and gimped to the door. I opened it about two inches. There was a revolver butt poised in the air, ready to hit again. I slammed the door faster than a jet plane takes off.

There was a roar from outside: "Hokay, hokay, Teed. It's only me. W'at you scare' of?"

Detective-Sergeant Framboise was now in this mess, whatever it was going to add up to.

For not the first time in the past few hours, I shrugged. I unlatched the door and shambled back to the living room. Framboise came in behind me. "You must be off duty, this time of day," I said. "The beer's in the frig."

I was sitting on the chesterfield when he came in from the kitchen. He had ignored the Dow pints at the front of the frig and burrowed in behind the milk to provide himself with a quart of Molson. Framboise, neatly dressed in a blue serge suit, with his hat still on and bottle and glass in his hands, looked quite the picture of the hearty, young French-Canadian heading for his table in a *taverne*. He had short legs and long arms and trunk, and walked with a roll, sort of like an ape who has served in the merchant marine. He had a hard, pasty face the color of unbaked bread and the consistency of a cemetery headstone. He was a bluff, blustery, emotional man, not half as smart as he thought he was but not at all dumb, either.

He sat down and poured his beer. Then he pulled out a large brown envelope he'd held tucked under his arm and spun it across the room to me. "I 'ave somet'ing there which may interes' you," he told me.

I opened the envelope. It was full of large photographs. I won't describe them in any detail, because they were a little nauseous. Besides that, they didn't show very much.

"You can't tell anything from these," I protested. "Have you got any 'before' pictures?"

He took a smaller studio print from an inside pocket and showed it to me. The man in the picture was past middle age, prosperous, smiling. He looked like a wealthy manufacturer or merchant. But he looked like a boy who had come up from sweeping the factory or the shop. There was hardness and the marks of a very rough life in the face, and the overlay of prosperity couldn't hide the cold determination in the eyes. 'I'm out for what's mine,' the eyes said.

"Don't tell me," I said. "I read about it. A guy found him dead on Mount Royal yestermorning."

"T'at's a new word," Framboise said delightedly. He took out a small, dirty notebook and a greasy pencil stub and painfully wrote 'yestermorning' on one of the pages. "Trying to himprove my Henglish," he said in explanation.

"Why come to me with this?" I put all the photographs back in the envelope, the shots of the bashed corpse and the one of the guy still alive, and skimmed it back across the room to him.

"Someone w'ispered to me t'at you might know 'im."

"I never saw him before. I don't know anything about him. I read the story in the papers, and before that I never heard his name before. I have about as much interest in him as you have in crimes committed on the front steps of the Kremlin in Moscow. I'm a private detective, like you so often have to remind me. I'm not interested in a case unless I get paid to work on it. You go ahead with your job. Have fun. I don't want any of it."

Framboise lifted his hands in a Gallic gesture of protest. He was drinking my beer, so he didn't get mad. And he wanted to stay there until he finished the quart, so he tried to explain.

"I'm honly trying to do my job. Someone said you might know somet'ing about 'im. I have to hask you."

"Who in hell told you that?"

"MacArnold."

"I might have known. Well, it's no go. I'm out of the case. And right now I've got a killer of a headache and I don't even want to hear about it."

"What's wrong?"

"Oh, I was slugged over the head last night. Two characters broke in here and worked me over."

"W'y? W'at you been doing lately?"

"Nothing," I said disgustedly. "And they didn't rob me."

Framboise got up to leave. "Then, w'y?" he said. "W'y?"

Chapter Five

WELL—W'y? It was a good question.

After Framboise left I went into the kitchen and whipped up a light lunch—the rest of the oysters, hamburger with green peas and little canned potatoes, which are the bachelor's friend; a cheese plate of Oka, Gruyere, Camembert and Roquefort; and coffee. I loaded it on a tray and went into the front room to eat.

Who was Lila-Delilah and why had she picked my apartment to pull her con act? Sure, I'd made it easy for her by thinking she was Elena and inviting her in, but she would have found some way to get the invitation. She knew my name, but that didn't mean anything—she could read it on my mailbox. And quite a few Montrealers knew I was a private eye after the last case hit the papers.

So she comes in, gets close enough to the front door alone to unlock it, and lets in her pals. I knew a lot of hoodlums around Montreal, but I'd never seen them before. Maybe they were imported talent—Toronto, perhaps, or Chicago. Chicago had been having a clean-up wave and a lot of unemployed hoods were arriving in the city from time to time.

While Delilah distracts me her pals sneak up behind and lay me out—that's the idea. Only the whisper of a sap saved me from that. But they mopped the floor with me in the end. So what was the purpose of it all? Straight theft?

It could have been. This was a nice apartment block. And the walls were thick enough to make a little robbery with violence perfectly possible. They could have cased the place and pinned on me, a guy who lived alone, obviously not poor, likely to have something worth taking.

There was only one thing wrong with that. They hadn't so much as snitched the T-bone steaks out of the frig. They hadn't even lifted my wallet from my pocket, after they had me lying there cold. And I don't care how scared they were after the noise of the battle, they would have waited for the wallet.

No, it wasn't robbery.

What was it? Maybe I'd been beaten up as a warning, but it was pretty foolish to do that and not warn me. Maybe they thought I had some inside information on a case in the place or on me, but if so they hadn't looked—and anyway, I wasn't on a case and I didn't have any inside dope on anything, not even the stock market. Maybe they thought I was dangerous to them and wanted to put me out of commission permanently—but sappers like that are too old at the game to leave a guy for dead unless he really is dead.

Any way I figured it out, it was screwy. I gave it up as a bad job and decided to go out and clear my head. I phoned my downtown garage. "Bert, I came home without my car last night. Today I'm in no condition to walk anywhere. Have it sent up, will you?" I instructed.

There was a gulp at the other end of the wire. An audible gulp, as the saying is.

"That's Mr. Teed, isn't it?" Bert asked.

"Sure."

"And yours is the black Riley roadster, Mr. Teed, isn't it?"

I didn't know why he was stalling, but he was. "Listen, Bert," I said, a little harshly, "you know bloody well the black Riley is mine. It's been mine for five years. Now, just have it sent up, like a good guy, eh?" I started to hang up.

Bert said, "Errr—"

"Well, what?"

"Honest, I don't know how to tell you, Mr. Teed. I was hoping you'd come by today so I could explain it to you."

The bottom fell out of my world. Something had happened to Riley. Riley was more than a car to me. He was my living chariot, my companion in solitude, my steed on swift flights through the night. My pride, my joy, my . . .

"Lord!" I breathed. "What happened? Come on, tell me. Did that manured farmer in your tow truck sideswipe Riley?"

"No sir. It's worse."

I sat down heavily in the chair beside the phone.

Bert said, "Your Riley's been stolen. I swear, Mr. Teed, it's the first time we lost a car in twelve years. The kid I had on night duty last night, he didn't know anything. A guy came in, said he was you, and the kid let him take Riley."

"Have you called the cops?"

"No, I called my insurance company. Don't worry, Mr. Teed, you'll get every cent if the car don't come back. And the kid, I already fired him. This morning."

"Wait a minute. If you weren't there, how did you know Riley was stolen? How did you know I didn't get the car myself?"

"Because the kid said you came in, late at night, and asked where your car was. That sounded suspicious, Mr. Teed; you know where we always park your car and you just go right down and get it. So I asked the kid to describe you. According to him you were over six foot tall, weighed about two hundred with shoulders like a truck driver, and had a meaty face with a jaw like the south end of a ship. That was when I called my agent. I didn't want to call the cops until I heard from you, but I was scared of what had happened. Do you want to call them, or will I?"

"I will," I said unhappily. The loss sat on me heavily as a curling stone on a toy balloon. It was the first time Riley and I had ever been parted. And when I though of that ham-handed, muscle-bound hood driving him . . .

"Mr. Teed," Bert said soothingly, "you want a car, I can send you up a car to drive right away. What would you like?"

"Oh, anything," I said disconsolately. "Well, anything convertible. You wouldn't happen to have another Riley?"

"Afraid not."

"An MG?"

"No. I tell you, I got a nice little green Morris Minor convertible."

"A *what*?"

"Morris Minor."

"Listen, remember me? I'm six feet tall. My knees would stick up through the spokes of the wheel and I couldn't steer the thing. And I hate to shift to low gear every time I go up a five degree incline."

"Now, Mr. Teed," Bert argued, "you know how to shift gears, with your Riley, to get the best out of the motor. You could drive this Morris up the side of a house if you know how to shift gears. And there's lots of room in 'em. I'm big, and I drive one."

"What else you got?"

"Nothing else in a convertible. Don't forget, these Morrises are made by the same company that makes Rileys. They're good little cars."

"Oh, all right," I said unhappily. "Send it up right away. And don't tell anyone else about the Riley being stolen, just yet."

"Why? Was the guy who picked it a friend of yours? "

"No, I wouldn't say so. But I have an idea who it was, and I'm going looking for him myself."

After a severe emotional shock like that, I needed something bracing. I got out the Seagram's VO bottle and poured myself a good hooker of rye. I didn't use water with it, but I put enough ice cubes to fill up the glass; that took three cubes.

I drank it and thought, things may be coming a bit clearer. For some reason, these thugs had a special purpose they wanted to use Riley for. So they put me out of circulation so they could go get Riley without any interference.

What were they going to do? Kill somebody with Riley and leave him on the scene so I'd get blamed? I shuddered.

The longer I thought, though, the more clear it became that you could reason it just the other way around. And if you reasoned it the other way, I wasn't any closer to a solution to the mystery of the attack on me than I'd been before.

Suppose, see, for some unknown reason these mugs want to heist me. They look into my life pretty carefully, and find out what they can about me, including what car I drive and where I keep it. So they slug me. Then they need a car for their getaway, or just to ride around in. What's more natural than to go put the finger on my car, when they knew I wouldn't be in shape to interfere?

So maybe the theft of Riley was an effect of the slugging, not the cause?

And now that you've limbered up your brain this far, Teed, what the hell *was* the cause, please? Well, we still didn't have any good ideas on that.

The buzzer downstairs at the front door was on a different circuit from the one at my doorway, and I hadn't smashed it in my blind morning rage. It whickered. I lifted the receiver on the call-box and a kid said, "Car from the garage."

"Okay. Leave it there with the keys."

I looked at my watch. I'd had lunch somewhere around four o'clock, and now it was about six. I looked up Jimmy

Montgomery in the book and dialled him.

"Hello," said his clipped voice.

"Montgomery? Russ Teed. Can I come out and see you for a few minutes?"

"Sure. I was just heating up the griller. I'll throw another chunk of beef on the fire for you."

"Thanks, I ate lunch too late to join you. If you've got beer on the ice you can shove in two or three more."

"Don't need to. I don't drink milk so there's always plenty cold. Come along."

"Right there," I said.

Well, I would have been, if I'd ever driven a Morris before. After I'd folded myself into the little bucket seat the size of a kid's toidy-chair I got it started all right, but going up Cote des Neiges from my place I guess I forgot I wasn't driving Riley. I shifted too quickly, and the little motor labored and then stalled. When I pulled the starter button the starter spring jammed. I had to back into a drive, start coasting downhill and let out the clutch before I could get the motor to catch. Then I turned around and came up Cote des Neiges again—this time in low, all the way.

Ridgewood Avenue cuts up from Cote des Neiges, opposite the big Catholic cemetery, and climbs up and around the hindquarters of Westmount Mountain in a crescent, ending at the back of Brother André's Shrine. Get high up on the crescent and you have a nice view—the Université de Montréal, the Town of Mount Royal and the suburbs beyond. It's a view to the north and east, rather than the south-east view from my own terrace that looks down on the main business heart of Montreal. But Montgomery's apartment building, the Gordon Arms, was high on Ridgewood and I began to expect he was a kindred soul.

I felt that even more strongly when he let me in. The

rooms were a bit small and boxy, but the apartment was neat and well-dressed, as though it felt the touch of a charwoman's hand a few times a week, the way mine did. I caught a glimpse of a grey and red living room as a I walked through, and then we went into a kitchen remarkably like mine. Even to the fact that the two large cupboards, which women always use for china and glass, were split evenly between glass and liquor. Even to the fact that the beer bulging out of the frig was Molson.

Montgomery was halfway through a thick sirloin steak on the kitchen table. I helped myself to a beer at his suggestion and drank it slowly while he chawed. I noticed he hadn't bothered to cook himself potatoes, and I told him where he could buy the little canned ones. This touched off a spark of real enthusiasm, and we discussed bachelor cooking right through coffee.

Then he said, "Well, what's up? I thought you weren't interested in the case of the body on Mount Royal?"

"I'm not. But I'm afraid the case may be interested in me. I got slugged last night. I've been trying to figure out why. More and more it seems to me it might have some connection."

"How come?"

I explained how I'd tried to figure why I *was* beat-up, and got nowhere, unless it was maybe because the bums wanted to swipe Riley. "Now I'm starting at the other end of the problem," I said. "Maybe I can figure out *who* pulled the job—or I mean, who hired the kids to pull it."

"Maybe the guys who shoved in Chesterley's head?"

"This is it," I said. "Until yesterday afternoon, I'm completely clean. I haven't been on a case for two months. All my old cases, I've been very careful to tidy up. No loose ends hanging around, unless you want to count Crawfie

Foster—we'll get to him later.

"So, early in the afternoon, I read about the Chesterley job in the paper. Then MacArnold calls me up to come to the Trafalgar. He obviously wants to interest me in the case. As I found out later, he even told Sergeant Framboise I was tied in with it. From the way we talked in the Traf, somebody listening might have thought I was going to work on the case. Later, a decoy-gal and two sap-swinging muscle-lugs visit me to discourage me from playing too active a part."

"You think they'd do that?"

"It's possible."

"I don't know you well enough to say it, but," Montgomery told me frankly, "you might be just a little conceited, you know."

"Oh, sure," I said sarcastically. "You just tell me why I got slugged, then."

"What else have you done since yesterday morning?"

"I drank beer in the Elephant Tavern. Alone. I found out Crawfie Foster was back in town—you heard MacArnold tell me. That could be the second possibility, and there I'm not being conceited. Crawfie knows what I'd do to him. If a friend of his overheard what I said in the Trafalgar, maybe Crawfie found out and set the gunsels on me."

"That sounds more like it. What else?"

"Well, there's a third—no, it isn't even a possibility. The guy would have to be telepathic. I met an old acquaintance, Paul Hanwood, just at the doorway of the bar. Maybe you saw it. He was with a girl. If he could read minds he'd know how I planned to work on that girl, and he would have told the rough boys to go kill me."

"I know what you mean. I saw the girl. What makes you think he'd have to read your mind? Maybe just your face."

"Okay, so it's a possibility," I said. "But aside from

that, somebody who was sitting near us in the Trafalagar overheard us talk, and that led to my broken head. Now—who was around there?"

Montgomery scowled, and in what seemed a characteristic gesture, rubbed his forehead with the heel of his hand, fingers pointing upward, cigarette smoking from his fingers. "Give me a minute," he said. "I think I can visualize it. I sat staring around for a few minutes, there, after MacArnold went to sleep and before you came in."

He bent his head and buried himself in thought, like a duck groping down through muddy water for tasty root. I opened the frig and got us two more quarts and uncapped them.

"Uh-huh," he said in a while, with satisfaction. He glanced over the table and picked up the sugar bowl. Dumping cubes over the table, he set up his diagram of the Trafalgar bar room. First sugar cube: "We were sitting here." Second cube: "Here, to our right, three girls—maybe young matrons—at another curved banquette. Expensively dressed, had been shopping—chattered about it. Society types."

"Remember the girl that came to the door, the one I met? Did one of the girls sitting near us look like her?"

"No, not enough for me to remember, anyway." He set up the third cube. "This was a small table at our left. Two men were sitting at it, talking business. You never saw two who looked less like crooks. One was slender and oldish, with pure white hair and bright blue eyes. He was dressed in the kind of suit I'd like to be able to buy. The younger one was maybe thirty-five. He had a face like a pansy—a bit puffy, and curly around the edges—if you can imagine an off-white pansy. He had very fine light-brown hair, thin on top, and rimless glasses."

"Oh, fine," I said. "Did you happen to hear what business

they were in?"

"Importing woollens."

"And you got all this without being particularly interested in them?"

"I was bored," he said. "I didn't have anything else to do but look at them. And my memory's fairly good."

"I wish Associated Chemical would fire you," I told him. "I'd be able to use you in my work. I'd pay you any salary you named."

He gave me a thin-lipped grin. "You couldn't meet the wage they give me. I'm their little expert."

"Yeah. Who's conceited now, may I ask?"

"I wouldn't kid. I'm the design expert on electrolytic process equipment. If they didn't have me, every time they wanted to build a new electrolysis plant they'd have to get a consulting firm up from the States and pay them fifty thousand. So it's good business to have me around at ten thou a year. None of my plants have fallen apart yet. I don't keep busy all the time, but I'm there when wanted."

"I see. Sometime you must tell me all about electrolysis. Sometime, but not now. Right now tell me if anyone else was in earshot of our talk at the Trafalgar."

"Unless you want to count the waiters, not a soul."

"That's swell. I'm still right where I was, unless your wispy-haired pansy had a gun concealed under each arm."

"He didn't. I would have noticed."

"How thick do you think you can make—" I began, before I realized he was kidding me. Then we both laughed together.

"I hope MacArnold got more out of you than I did," I told him. "I don't know what he was after, but I hope he got something for his expense money."

"Nope. I didn't know anything I didn't tell the cops and

the other reporters."

"I wonder what he thinks he can pull up on this?"

"He seemed to have an idea Chesterley was in a gambling set-up. He was going to work on that today, he said. Did you see the *Clarion* this morning?"

"I sure didn't."

"There was nothing new on the case. The police had said nothing except that they weren't issuing any statement on it for at least two days. That leaves MacArnold some time to work on a beat."

"Yep. Now that I'm getting interested, I think maybe I'll work on MacArnold. Got a phone?"

"Right there in the hall."

I called the *Clarion* but he hadn't reported for work yet. I tried his home number, then the Jamaica Cafe, and finally got him at Louie Two's Bar.

"Hi," I said. "How are you doing on the Chesterley job?"

"I thought you weren't interested. In fact, Framboise tells me you were so uninterested you almost threw him out on his prat."

"He always gets sore when he leaves my place after only one quart. Things have changed, anyhow. I might be interested."

"Either you are or you aren't."

"All right, I am."

"Okay. Chesterley was one of three partners in a flossy gambling set-up, until the time of his unfortunate walk across the mountain."

"Do the cops know? Has Framboise got this?"

"I don't think so. Louie Two's is the only place you can get information like this, so far as I know, and Framboise hasn't had any of these boys on the griddle. I haven't told him. He isn't so good a friend of mine he can't spend a nickel to read it in the *Clarion*."

"Who are the other two in the dice-joint?"

"Not dice. Big stuff—mostly roulette, and formal dress to get by the peeper at the door. All that. One of the other partners is a guy called Irish Joe. I gather he's an uncultured type who operates any unpleasant parts of the business. The third partner is just a rumor. No one knows who he is, but Louie Two swears he exists because the boys came into his back room one night to split up the take, and they split it three ways."

"That's nice. Well, where do we find the only known surviving partner?"

"Behind the roulette wheel, I suppose, if we could find it. The location is a secret. That's what's holding me up."

"Louie Two knows, I suppose."

"Sure, but he won't tell."

"How hard have you tried him? Fifty bucks? Add another fifty from me. He'll talk for a century."

"He won't talk for anything. They closed the lights and locked the door in this place when Chesterley was bumped. They figure to stay closed until the heat's off—for certain. Louie Two won't give me the combination until he gets the word they're open for business again. Claims it's a matter of honor, and a grand wouldn't open his yap."

"Well, when do they take off the wraps again?"

"It's better than you think. Maybe tonight."

"Let's go there together."

"Sure," MacArnold said, and there was a note of relief in his voice. "Happy to have you. I'll call you at your place."

"I'm not at my place, and I don't know when I'll get back. I better call you. Are you staying at Louie Two's?"

"You bet I am. I got dispensation from Hatch, so I don't have to show up at the shop. Long as I'm chasing this story, he doesn't care where I am."

"Okay. I'll phone you every hour," I told him, and rang off.

Montgomery had wandered into the hall with a glass in his hand and was listening idly. "Sounds like something might be popping," he commented.

"Could be."

"I'm free tonight. And I love trouble."

"Okay. We can't do much until MacArnold gives the word. Meanwhile, I've got a little investigating to do in another matter. I want to put a tape on Crawfie Foster, if I can."

"Does this involve going someplace where we can drink?"

"It does."

Montgomery raised his full glass to his lips and again performed the feat I'd noticed once before, in the Trafalgar. He simply opened his epiglottis, elevated the glass and the beer was on a non-stop trip to his stomach. "Okay, let's go," he said.

Chapter Six

WITH THE EXCEPTION of one short steep climb, it was downhill all the way from Montgomery's place on Ridgewood to the centre of town. The Morris Minor romped along, sneaking in and out among the other cars and exhibiting lots of pep if you remembered to change down at curves and corners. I even began to feel a little affectionate toward it. Compared to Riley it was as a romping puppy is to a race horse, with about as much comparative power; but it was frisky. We cruised along the parking strip behind the Dominion Square Building, at the edge of Dominion Square, and stopped at a crevice between two cars.

"One thing," I said with satisfaction, "you can park these little babies anywhere."

Montgomery craned his neck. "Sorry. You can't have that spot. There's a motorcycle parked there."

We circled again. A Chevrolet started up and moved away and we went in, leaving enough room for a second Morris besides.

I led Montgomery across St. Catherine and into the Elephant Tavern. He glanced around. "Haven't been in here before. Our office is farther east, and we frequent the oasis nearest the shop."

"It's just like any other Montreal tavern," I said. For no good reason I felt poetic. "It's got the same dark wood walls, smoked black from the fumes of a billion cigarettes. It's got colored glass in the front window so women, who can't come in, can't even see into the last haunt of the male. People sit here all day and swill beer and if they can still sit in their chairs they get served. If they go to sleep with their heads on the tables the waiters let them lie quietly. You can spill beer and knock glasses or even bottles on the floor, and nobody will care much—it's your beer, the glasses are cheap, and the floors are made of terrazzo and can take it. You can start a fight, and the waiters are strong enough to throw you out. The only unforgivable sin is starting a sing-song. I don't like that; I think pubs are meant for sing-songs. But in Montreal, singing is a disturbance and it brings the cops. And nobody likes cops in taverns—when they're on duty."

"'S true," said Montgomery, unimpressed by the rhapsody. "Two quarts of Molson!"

Harry brought the Molson down the long, narrow room. I caught the check, with a two-dollar bill. "Keep the change, Harry," I said.

He looked at me with raised brows. "This is a two."

"That is a two, all for you, woo-woo," I said. It came out unintentionally and sounded silly as hell, and I realized I must have stacked up one or two over the airport at Montgomery's, and they were coming in for a landing now. "The two is because I love you. And because you're a bright character who has his eyes open. And because you serve the tables at the front of this grog shop and can see out the front door. Tell me, what were you doing on May thirty-first?"

"If it was a week day, I was here."

"Did you happen to notice a moving van, or moving truck, parked just outside the front door?"

"What time?"

Oh—early afternoon, probably."

"I come on at six p.m.," Harry said. He politely wiped the table clean in front of us, and walked away.

Montgomery snickered. "That's a good way to spend money."

I fixed him with a squinty glare. "MacArnold has always

been my friend and severest critic, but you're developing into an acceptable substitute. Come on, let's leave."

We downed our beer and went out. A doorway beside the tavern front gave on a flight of stairs to the offices on the floor above. The door was unlocked.

It was an old building. We climbed worn treads in a narrow stairwell with nauseous green walls on either side of us, the peculiarly griping color they use to make old walls brighter. Upstairs we were in a wide hallway with an almost-black old wooden floor and glaring ceiling lights. On either side of the hall was a row of glass-panelled doors, each inscribed with some legend. I walked down the row until I hit one labelled Foster Fotos, in florid script.

"They haven't rented his studio again, anyhow," I remarked. Montgomery joined me. I tried the door, and it was locked.

"What now, private eye? Skeleton keys?"

"Nah. They're out of fashion."

Nobody was around. I took a strip of rigid celluloid, two inches wide and a foot long, from my breast pocket. I worked it in easily between the door and the jamb, just above the latch, and then sawed down and inward. The latch slid back and the door fell ajar. "The old places are easy. A client showed me that."

We went in. Montgomery said, "By the way, who's your client in the Chesterley case?"

"I'm my own client. I'll transfer five hundred moidores from the front to the back pocket when I find out who sicced the sluggers on me."

Inside, the rooms were a shambles. There was a small outer room, and then the darkroom with its sinks and tables and black walls, with the clinging sick-sweet smells of developer and hypo. All around, but mostly on the floor, was scattered the offal of a deserted photographic shop. Spoiled prints, torn folders, negatives in all sizes and stages of repair, film packs, holders; junk. I kicked at it with my feet. There was lots of evidence there that Crawfie had been taking night club pics, but there wouldn't be any clue to his new location. I didn't really expect it, I guess.

I went back to the outer room and looked quickly through the drawers of the desk. They were clean—too clean, as if he had scooped these out really carefully while letting the rest of the place be cleaned by the movers.

Just on spec, I began taking out the drawers. It was an old desk, solidly built, and each drawer was set in its own individual compartment. In a lower right-hand drawer I found a bit of paper had shoved up to the top of the drawer when it was full, been caught by the upper frame when the drawer was pulled out and had dropped in behind, to lie underneath the drawer until I found it.

It wasn't much. It was a photograph, only snapshot size, of a man—coat and hat on—stepping through an open apartment doorway, apparently out of the apartment into the corridor of the building. The man wasn't anybody I recognized, and I sure as heck didn't recognize the apartment door. But on the other hand, this was part of Crawfie's private life. It was no night club shot. It might be worth something some time.

I showed it to Montgomery.

"Nope. Never saw him. Looks a little like that Man of Distinction just after he drank the glass he's been holding for the last few years."

"That old gag," I snorted. "Well, that's all. When we clear out of here we can go back and drink again, and phone MacArnold to see how he's doing."

"Let's pass the tavern. I feel like paying more for my beer

and sitting in a place where I can see girls at the next table."

I didn't protest, so he took me to the Alamo, one of the little upstairs clubs along St. Catherine east of Peel. This one was tricked out like an old time Texas saloon, with leather (fake) and weather-beaten wood (fake) everywhere except on the floor. The waiters wore leather vests and the cigarette girl had on a cowboy suit, complete except for pants and chaps.

I called MacArnold, and MacArnold had no news, and then we sat down at the table and right away we had a table-hopper. I was surprised. It was a type who didn't usually hop tables.

It was Paul Hanwood.

"Hyah, Paul," I said. "Not alone, I hope?" I'm usually a little more subtle, but I was on my seventh quart, as close as I could count, not including the rye in memoriam of Riley.

"Yes, I was sitting at the bar," he said pleasantly.

"Join us?"

"Thanks, I'm waiting for someone. I'll sit down for just one quick one."

I introduced him to Montgomery. We ordered beers and he had a brandy Alexander which, if you want my opinion, is a chocolate milk-shake with a sniff of cheap grog mixed in.

"Haven't I met you before, Mr. Montgomery?" he asked, looking at Jimmy intently.

"I was sitting with Mr. Teed yesterday afternoon when you came into the Trafalgar."

"Ah, yes. And MacArnold. Are you mixed up in this business of the body on Mount Royal, too?"

"I found it."

"Oh! Yes, of course, I read your name in the newspaper account. Tell me, Russell, how's the case coming?"

"How should I know?" I asked crossly. "I'm not on it. I haven't a client."

"Intriguing crime. The body wasn't robbed. Sounds like a revenge killing, or somebody's mouth being shut, doesn't it?"

"Yes, Mr. District Attorney," I grunted.

I glanced around the room and let Montgomery take him on for a while. I just wasn't interested in Hanwood when he didn't have Elena Giotto with him.

There was a bright flash over in a far corner, and I squinted that way. A small gal with dark hair was shooting an entwined couple at a table along the wall. She gave the guy his claim check and turned toward me, and I saw it was Priscilla Dover.

I got up and threaded my way through the tables toward her.

"Hello," I said in greeting. "You didn't tell me you were still working this racket. Got a new boss?"

She looked at me carefully. She stole glances to left and right. Life, love, drinking and smoking of straight and blended cigarettes was going on at the tables around us, and no one was throwing so much as a tinker's damn in our direction.

When she spoke it was barely more than a whisper. "Hello, Mr. Teed. Yes, I'm working for Clancy Photos now. He has the concession here."

She wouldn't meet my eye. She was even trying to look as though she weren't talking to me, but just waiting for me to move so she could get past.

She was scared to death of something.

"What's wrong?"

"I—I'll call you tomorrow."

"Look, something's the matter."

"I can't say anything here."

"Nobody's going to hurt you. Over my dead body, they would. If you want, we can go somewhere we can talk."

“I don’t want to be seen with you.”

“You’re frightened!”

At last she raised her eyes to mine. The pupils were dilated and the eyes were wide and a bit wild. She’d had a bad scare, or else just the fact of talking to me seemed terribly dangerous to her.

“I’ll call you tomorrow,” she said. “I can’t say just when. But I’ll call you. Please, wait for the call.”

“I will. But tell me now. Maybe I can help.”

She shook her head with a quick nervous little gesture. She brushed past me on her way to the door. “I’ve seen Foster again,” she whispered. “I’ll tell you the rest on the telephone.”

Chapter Seven

We stayed in the Alamo a long time. Paul Hanwood drifted away from our table after a while and went to the bar to meet his friend. I was sorry to see it was another man—not Elena. They put on a floor show of sorts, consisting mainly of a poor man's Gene Autrey. I think he was mainly Italian in background, and if he'd ever gone farther west than Chicago with his songs he'd have been shot as an insult to the wide open spaces.

Every hour I called MacArnold, and every hour he had nothing to report.

Montgomery and I got involved in a long and serious discussion of whether the practise of natural rhythm was strictly kosher for a married Catholic. Neither of us was married nor Catholic, so I don't know how we got on the subject. But it proved to be something we disagree about without feeling strongly enough to fight, so it passed the time. I found out more about him; he was a Montreal boy, from N.D.G., and he'd graduated in Chemical Engineering from McGill. He hadn't been there the same years I'd attended, so we didn't have any mutual acquaintances. His mother and father were dead but he had two married brothers in Montreal.

Just before I was due to make the one o'clock call to MacArnold, Montgomery pulled a yawn that would have encompassed a watermelon and said, "Well, this kid's had enough. I have to work tomorrow. Nothing's going to happen tonight."

"I think you're right. I'll call Mac and tell him he can phone me at the apartment. Then I'll drive you home."

It was a long, slow ride home. Morris Minors are fine in

flat country, or if you can arrange to be going down hill all the time, but when you have to climb I'll take a good strong horse in preference.

I got back home and put the Morris in the garage in my apartment block. Then I wandered wearily up to my own little cave, smothering yawns on the way. This kid was pretty beat, too. Besides, my bad leg was getting stiffer than a plaster cast and my head had started to ache again.

So I got inside my door and there was MacArnold on the phone, before I had time to turn the lights on.

"It came through!" he gloated.

"It would," I sighed.

"Louie Two just got word they opened up for business late this evening. They're even looking for customers. And he told me the address."

"Where is the place?"

"Want to guess?"

"All the high-class gambling joints in the city—and most of the crummy ones—are away out of town. On the roads north or west. They're isolated houses, with space for concealed parking. So this place is, let's see, maybe a big house in St. Laurent?"

"You couldn't be wronger. In the first place, it isn't even a house. It's just an apartment. And it's so far in the centre of town it's nearer me than you right now."

"Where?"

"On Sherbrooke Street." He named the number.

"That's about a block west of McGill University, on the lower side of the street, isn't it? I'll be damned! Foxy. So close to downtown the cops wouldn't think of suspecting it there. And a crowd of cars parked on Sherbrooke Street late at night wouldn't attract anybody's attention—except a traffic prowler giving out tickets."

"Right. Well, are you coming?"

"I guess so. Wait for me on the corner of Sherbrooke and Mansfield. I'll be there as soon as you can walk it from Louie Two's." I rang off, picked up the keys to the Morris, and started out the door. Then I changed my mind and slung the keys back on the hall table. To hell with trying to drive a strange and balky car at this time of the morning. I'd get a taxi.

When we met on the corner it was just two a.m. "They should be well underway about now," MacArnold said.

"Should be. How do we get in?"

"Tell 'em Louie Two sent us. He's one of their streeters."

The apartment block was a big one, maybe fifteen stories tall, yellow brick and perfectly square. It had been built a good thirty years before, but built to stay. Perhaps ten years before it had still been luxury accommodation—eight and ten room apartments with at least two bathrooms, maids' quarters, and walls and floors thick enough to keep out noise. Now it was an old-fashioned place, and people who were wealthy but liked apartment life had moved further up the hill. The cards on the mail boxes showed who lived here now—most of the apartments were shared, sometimes with as many as six names for one number. Business girls, nurses, bachelors; one or two college fraternities. The number we wanted was sixteen; the card said simply KILLROY.

MacArnold eyed it in silence. "I'm trying to make a good gag about that," he explained, "like 'Killroy sure wasn't here yesterday.' But it just won't come."

There was no lock on the entry door. We went in and crawled into a minute self-service elevator that took us to the eighth floor.

There was a small, almost square corridor, and the only two apartments on the floor—fifteen and sixteen—spread off to front and back of the building, respectively, their doors sitting on opposite sides of the corridor and glaring at each other.

We buzzed, and the door of sixteen opened—on a chain.

MacArnold faced the crack. "Louie Two sent me," he said. "I got a pal with me."

There was a pause, and I guess Mac was getting a once-over. Then a rough voice said, "Take yer hat off, brother. You ain't applying for admission to a flophouse." Mac complied.

"Where's the other guy?"

I took the State Express out of my mouth and butted it tidily in a corner. I took off my hat, straightened my tie and smoothed back the hair. I stepped in front of the crack and said sweetly, "Will I do?"

The door opened. The watchdog was a short gorilla with almost as much hair as a sheep dog, but stiffer, and black. He was dressed faultlessly in full evening garb. He looked at MacArnold and indicated me with a scornful thumb. "Drunk, or does he think he's funny?"

"Where's the play?" Mac asked in a low voice.

The sheep dog gave him the cold eye. "This is a private club. Come over here and I'll fill out your membership cards."

MacArnold said he was John Hatch—his editor's name—and I told Happy Harry to put down Paul Hanwood on my card. He took the names without comment, wrote us up in his social register, and waved to the next room.

The room was fixed up like a small buffet-bar, or perhaps the snack room of a sportsman's club. At one side was long table covered with a gleaming linen cloth and loaded with everything from cold turkey through roast beef to caviar canapes. At the other side was a small, thoroughly-stocked bar. A few people ate and chatted, or drank and wept out their losses, at small tables. The only thing missing was a cash register; clearly, this was on the house.

MacArnold headed for the bar. They were going to lose money on him.

I pressed on. Through a heavy baize-padded door was a long, low, smoke-heavy room, thick of carpet and plastered with acoustic tile to cut the noise to a quiet roar. There were two roulette wheels, and there were two crap tables, and most of the people milling about were well dressed, but in street clothes. It was a high-class place, but not as high-class as MacArnold had been led to believe.

It was a large room—maybe they'd knocked out a wall between living and dining rooms in the apartment. It had to be large to accommodate the crap tables. Each was roughly the size of a ping-pong table. But they were higher than ping-pong tables, covered with green baize painted to indicate the plays, and fenced with sides that came about eight inches above the table tops. Each table was run by three men—one in the slot at the centre, and two end-men. Between the tables, sitting high on a chair like tennis match umpires use, was an expert who carefully watched the play for switched dice or phoney rolls, first eyeing one table and the other.

I edged in at the end of the near table. There were perhaps twenty players around it, and that didn't crowd your elbows. I took out my wallet and threw two twenties to the slot man. "Chips!" I called.

He grabbed my money, stowed it neatly in a cash box, and shot two yellow chips back to me.

Now I knew I was in a high-class joint.

He saw my face. "You're at the twenty end," he called to me. "You want to hoard your money, go round to the ten end of the table." I shook my head and stayed where I was.

It looked like an honest game—mainly because the house covered all bets, but you could bet either with or against the roller, with just enough odds against you so the house got its take by the laws of chance in the long run.

I saved my chips. I wasn't wasting twenty bucks on any side bets. Finally the guy next to me crapped out and passed the roll. The slot man snicked in the dice with long, thin cane, curved at the end, and stowed them in a box. He shoved the box toward me, offering me my choice of any two dice from the six in the box.

I shoved one of the expensive yellow chips out onto the WIN bracket, shook the babies until they were warm, and chucked them out so they bounced off the other wall of the table. They gave me six, the hard way.

It was a nice point, nice as you could ask for. It was a lucky first roll. I flipped another chip to the COME square, shook them out again, and they gave me snake-eyes. Crappo; there went the come money. The very next roll they naturaled, but of course they naturaled on a seven—which lost me my six point and my last chip. I shook my head very sadly. I was old enough to know better than this. I moved down the table past the centre and hit the slot man for some ten-dollar chips, and when the dice came back to me I made two passes, dragged on instinct, crapped, then made a pass on big dick. That gave me a hunch and I left it all out for three more passes. I dragged again and this time sevened trying to make little joe. I picked up and left the table, drunk with elation. I'd put seventy bucks into chips, counting the first sad twenties, and was now clacking two hundred little ivory men together in my pocket. It was good enough for one night.

I tapped the ankle of the guy on the high watch-bird chair. "Where'll I find Irish Joe?"

He had a green eyeshade, pasty face, and the coldest eyes you ever saw this side of a fish store. "You got a complaint?"

"Naw. Want to meet him. An old buddy of his back in Chi told me to look him up."

The watch-bird pointed. "Through that door, and state the details to the guy you'll meet just inside. Don't be funny with him in any way, 'cause he might misunderstand; his business is to keep Irish from subscribing to too many charities. He'll find out if Irish Joe wants to see you."

I threaded my way past him and between the crap tables toward the door he'd pointed out. I went through the door and after I'd closed it I was in a hallway lit by a bulb at least five watts strong. You could hardly see a lighted cigarette in front of your face. It was a minute before my eyes tuned themselves to the dim light and showed me the corridor was short, and had one door at its end, and a man standing in front of the door.

Man, I said. Well, he was approximately a man. He was scrawny and not tall, and he held his arms nervously out from his sides as though he was paid to wait there for something to happen, and things kept happening all the time.

I walked toward him, and then I could see that his face was swathed in bandages. His eyes peeped through and there was a small hole designed for eating, drinking and smoking, but the rest of him was gauzy as an Egyptian mummy from the neck up.

"Yeah?" he said, and I didn't like his voice.

"The watcher told me I'd find Irish Joe in here."

"Who wants him?"

"Tell him Iggy the Spick sent me."

I used a name that was likely to get results. It was a name on a lot of lips in Chi, not too long ago. It was a name a lot of lips whispered before they stiffened for keeps, and it commanded a good bit of respect. Even the bandage-puss knew what it meant, and didn't bother to argue.

He opened the door behind him, snaking a hand back to do it and still watching me carefully. As the door swung, a stronger light fell on my face.

The guy froze. He dropped his hand off the doorknob, not even bothering to pull it shut again. He didn't waste time on words, either. He just gathered himself in, grabbed for something in his breast pocket, and sprung at me.

I didn't know whether the walls were thick enough so they could use guns in here, but I didn't wait to find out. I didn't have one myself, and I was never a guy who would enjoy a duel with a wet washcloth against a tommy gun at five paces. I cut and ran, and he was hard after me but not hard enough to keep me from opening the door to the game-room.

I was back in the smoky, crowded bright lights again, and the crap tables were between me and the door to outside.

I looked back briefly, and he was still coming. He didn't seem to give a damn if he made a scene in a semi-public place or not.

And he was the guy I thought he was, too.

I bore on at a harried lope between the dice tables, and the watch-bird on the high-chair was square in my way. And the boy with the mummy-face almost had me by the coat collar. I grabbed the high-chair and pulled hard, ducking at the same time.

The high-chair went right over my back, and as it angled out into space the watcher half jumped, half fell, sideways onto the middle of the left crap table. The tabletop must have been cheap plywood because I heard him crash through. I bet he broke up the game at that table.

The chair itself was pretty solid carpentry and when

it landed on the bandage-puss he went over on his back underneath it. I scrambled to my feet and walked at a comfortable pace to the outer door. Either they didn't have extra guards in here, or they were poorly spotted. Sometime after things calmed down I'd come back and tell Irish Joe about it, and charge him the usual consulting fee.

By the time I got to the green-baize padded door, a lot of the well-dressed women around were proving they could scream as loud as their coarser sisters. But the men were all frozen in their spots, not making a false move. They knew trouble when they saw it, and none of them wanted any.

I opened the door and stepped through, and when it shut behind me I was in the calmest, quietest room in the city. The boys who designed that place knew their acoustics. There were still a few people in the little buffet-bar, and of course there was still one Allan MacArnold sitting at the bar, lapping.

I tapped his shoulder. With one finger, yet, I almost knocked him off the stool. "Nunghg?" he mouthed.

"Time we went, Junior."

"Whaddya fin' out?"

"That I wasn't welcome here."

The green baize door shot open. In front of MacArnold was a large, heavy glass half full of drink. I picked it up and heaved, and it was a good pitching night. I got bandage-puss right in the middle of the bandage, and he staggered back through the door. It slammed again in front of him.

I grabbed MacArnold's hand and yanked him off the stool and out of the room, like kids playing snap-the-whip.

"Y' didn' have to take my drink away," he grumbled. "'M not *that* drunk."

"I needed it," I said briefly, "more than you did."

I slowed us down to a walk going through the entry in

case the little watch-dog was around, but we didn't even see him. I snapped the safety chain off the door, pulled it open and we were out.

I thought of stairs right away—we couldn't afford to wait for any elevators. But the little self-service job was sitting right there and all we had to do was get in—and get out of the building.

By the time we were on the street, MacArnold's last swallow had infiltrated his blood stream and I had to half-carry him to the nearest all-night coffee stand. Three cups of black coffee later, he had one eye open and about half his brain roused, and it was possible to begin explaining things to him.

"Things are beginning to fit in," I said.

"Sure. Was a nice plashe," he told me. "Free drinksh."

"Only because they don't cater to newsmen usually. Come on, wake up," I said, and kicked him hard on the shin-bone.

"Ouch! Okay, okay."

"You know who I saw in there?"

"Who wants to play riddle-games this time of morning?"

"The guy," I said, "who tried to sap me in my own apartment. Old mahogany face. And one gets you five that means Irish Joe was the other lug who busted in my place—the muscle man with the anthracite jaw."

"So, good. You wanted a tie-in between you and the body on the mountain, didn't you. Now you happy? Will you work on the case?"

"I sure will."

"Fine. Let's work on it tomorrow afternoon, then."

Purely out of pity for him I loaded him in a taxi and dumped him off at his Shuter Street apartment on my way home. When I got back to my place, it wasn't even five a.m.

yet. I yawned and began undressing.

It looked as if things were stacking up, even if I didn't have a client yet. The evening was an unqualified success.

Oh-oh. Except for one thing. When I emptied my pockets I realized something horrible had happened. In my pants pocket was two hundred dollars in little red chips, that I'd never redeemed.

They weren't worth two hundred bucks anywhere outside Irish Joe's. And I wasn't going there any more.

Chapter Eight

I WOKE UP, and it seemed like time to wake up. I'd come out of my dreams without outside stimuli. My phone wasn't ringing, the buzzer wasn't gargling, no one was hammering on my door. A more religious man would have made a novena. I reached for a cigarette.

My lungs still thick with last night's smoke, my teeth coated and my tongue furry with tar, my ulcers whimpering for food—I reached for a cigarette. Some guys get used to waking up in a set routine; I wake up with a cigarette. And has to be State Express.

Not, mind you, that I couldn't smoke Exports or Players and get the same taste. You get used to a brand. I got used to a brand with a light colored package, because my business takes me to lots of places where a boy who whips out a little notebook is automatically suspect. But nobody objects to an absent-minded soaker grabbing his pen and scribbling on the back of a cig pack. That's what I do. Of course, I lose a lot of notes, but some stay with me until I can use them.

Like the one word I'd printed in big letters on the back of last night's State Express box: PRISCILLA.

I looked at that, and then leaned back comfortably in bed again. All I had to do today was wait around for the phone to ring. After the last few days, it was a pleasant thought.

A less pleasant item of information was lying on my bedside stand. It was my watch; three o'clock, it said.

I got up slowly and wandered to the kitchen and cooked brunch. I started with a few eggs, but they just whetted my appetite, so I made a good corned beef hash—the secret is to have lots of cold boiled potatoes, a couple of days old, chop them up fine into the corned beef, and be sure to leave the skins on.

I polished that off. I felt a lot less dilapidated.

To hell with waiting around all day for Priscilla Dover to call me. She and the whole Crawfie Foster business were something I wanted to get cleaned up and out of the way, so I could concentrate on linking the little monkey with the mahogany face, and Irish Joe, to the slaying of Chesterley.

I let my mind dwell on that for a minute, and I got a picture that seemed clear as far as it went. First, I'd always thought the mountain job was done by two men—one to hold and one to slug. Supposing the rock-faced muscle boy was Irish Joe, I would pick him for the holder and the little brown monkey as the slugger. Monkey had held his sap in his right hand when he came after me, and the guy who killed Chesterley was right-handed; that wasn't conclusive, but it was corroborative detail.

These guys have slugged Chesterley because he is their partner in the gambling joint—this is making another assumption, that Monkey is the unknown third partner. They slug him because he argues with them about the cut, or disagrees on matters of policy—or perhaps only because they know he walks on the mountain alone, and they are tired of splitting three ways.

The afternoon after the slaying, I wander into the Trafalgar and a casual listener might conclude I was being brought into the case. Some pal of Irish Joe's overhears, and reports. Maybe I am conceited if I think that scares them; maybe they just didn't want anybody at all interested in the murder. Anyway, they dream up the play with Delilah—not to warn me, and not to kill me, I'd figured out before. Perhaps they figure the wallops will put me out of commission for a few weeks, and I'm a little tougher than they thought.

So that cleared that up, as far as it went. They go back to their apartment casino, and after a day feel safe enough to open for business again. And what can I do about it? Because I have about enough proof of anything to convict a Great Dane of liking beefsteak.

Sure, I could tell Framboise about Chesterley being a partner in the gambling joint, along with Irish Joe and Monkey, and that would get them hauled in and shaken out, and then off they'd go again, wiser and more cagey. Telling Framboise was a last resort of last resorts.

Which left me with the case still on my hands, and one very interesting problem to delve into. I was damned sure that neither Monkey not Irish Joe had been in the Trafalgar the time I went there to meet MacArnold. So who was there who told them?

For a minute a glancing, dirty suspicion crossed my mind. It was so dirty I went and brushed the shreds of corned beef out of my teeth, and dismissed it.

And then I had to get the Priscilla Dover business on the rails before I went on with Chesterley.

What was the name? Clancy Photos, I thought she'd said she worked for now. I looked in the yellow pages and found them. I phoned and it rang about ten times.

Somebody finally picked the croaker off its cradle to shut it up, and I said, "Clancy Photos?"

"Yeah?"

"Does a Miss Dover work for you?"

"I'm the janitor, Mac. These people only work at night."

I went through all the Dovers in the book after that. There were six. Four of them answered their phones, and none of the four owned anyone named Priscilla.

I scratched my head. I touched the soft spot, which was beginning to heal nicely, and came away with blood on my nails and wished I hadn't scratched my head. On a last dim hope, I called MacArnold.

When I got him out of his sack I said, "Remember the gal you sent around to me? The little photo-gal who'd been having trouble with Crawfie Foster?"

"Yeah."

"Know where she hangs out?"

"Yeah. Clancy Photos."

"No, no, dammit. When she's home."

"No."

"Okay, forget it."

"But I got her number. Wait." He went away, probably to scramble through the mouse's nest of old envelopes he kept in his jacket pocket, and came back. "It's either one of these two numbers," he said, and rhymed them off.

So I called them both; so they both didn't answer. But one seemed familiar. I looked in the book again, and it was one of the Dovers who hadn't answered before. That was fine. That gave me the address, and I was ripe to investigate it.

She lived down on MacKay Street, the one next to Guy, below Sherbrooke and just above St. Catherine. I cruised until I came to the number and then nosed to the curb, stepped on the brakes, and cracked my forehead on the windshield of the Morris as I stopped. Me and my big flat feet.

It was an old brick house, an undetached house squeezed in between two others and high and narrow, as though its neighbors had been shouldering it in and up for decades.

It was an old residence made into apartments, and there were mail boxes in the vestibule—her name, S. P. Dover, was on No. 3—and no lock on the front door. I went in and found No. 3 at the back of the ground floor.

I would have rung her bell, but I noticed her door was ajar.

Some kind of suspicion stirred in my mind, and produced the usual physical effects. My glands started spitting adrenalin into my alcoholic old bloodstream and my knees twiddled, my back crawled, my whole body got tense and squeezed sweat out through my pores.

I don't like doors ajar.

I went back to the Morris and got the largest spanner I could find out of the trunk.

The gal had been scared when she saw me the night before. That might mean something, or nothing. The unlatched door might mean something, or nothing. But Teed was gripping a spanner in his hand, and sure as hell he wished it was a gun.

I came to her door again. I didn't ring; I don't like trouble well enough to give it fair warning I'm coming. I went quietly in.

It was only a one-room apartment, and I could see her as I stole through the doorway. The light wasn't good; the place was still made up for the night, with blinds drawn and the day bed opened up and spread with bedclothes.

And she was on the bed. Very still.

I groped for the light switch, and didn't get it. I strode to the window and snapped up the blind. Then I went back to look at her and it was a full minute before I realized I was still foolishly holding the useless spanner in my hand.

She was lying very peacefully on her back in the bed, the covers shoved down to her waist. She was dressed in a very plain little pair of pyjamas, white with blue piping. Her eyes were closed. She looked about fifteen years old, with her short dark hair pushed out around her head on the pillow.

There was a puddle of blood, about as much blood as you would expect one person to hold, spreading out from under her left arm and filling all the hollow in the mattress made by her body, down the left side.

I knelt beside the low bed. I touched her wrist; there wasn't any pulse. There wasn't enough blood left to be pulsing. I lifted her arm, and it moved almost naturally, not stiff at all. Her flesh was warm. She hadn't been shot long ago.

I unbuttoned the pyjama coat and laid it gently back. She had small, girlish breasts and her skin was very white. There was a smallish, blackened bullet hole below her left breast, and some blood had trickled down and over her side; but most of the blood must have come from the back, where the bullet came out.

She was absolutely still and not breathing; or anyway you couldn't detect it. Her eyes were closed and when I open one lid, all I could see was white. And no pulse. But maybe she wasn't quite dead. Maybe she could be saved.

I put my ear down to her chest. At first I couldn't hear anything, but after an interminable wait I sensed a stirring.

Her heart was still beating. Weakly and slowly, but beating.

That was when I had to tell myself to keep calm. I jumped away from her and wanted to go six directions at once—go running out to the street, shouting, break a fire alarm box . . .

A phone. There had to be a phone here in the room. Sure. It was on a little desk, by the door, at the foot of the bed.

I only have a few numbers memorized, but one that's stood me in best stead is Danny Moore's. I dialled, and thanked God that his switch wasn't turned onto TAS. His own secretary answered, and something in my voice when I said, "Give me Danny, fast," made her run into his office for him. He was on the line before I could draw a deep breath.

"Russ Teed, Danny," I said, and told him clearly where I was. Then I said, "I have a girl here, shot below the heart, probably through the lung. Lost most of her blood, but still alive. Get your girl going on an ambulance, and make sure they bring plasma."

I could faintly hear a pencil scratch, and I imagined him noting, "Ambulance—plasma" below the address on his note pad, and sending the girl to the other phone with it.

"Okay," he said quietly. "They'll bring oxygen, too. Is the bullet inside her?"

"I think it went through."

"Likely means surgery, anyway, if she can take it. I'll set up an operating room and get Tyler or Fish—chest work isn't my baby. This may be a matter of minutes, right now. How's respiration?"

"Not noticeable."

"Heart?"

"Pretty spotty."

"Hold on. Don't touch her. I'm just around the corner from you. I'll likely be there before the ambulance."

At that, it was a tie. The ambulance screamed up from St. Catherine, and Danny galloped down from Sherbrooke and they met at the door. I was waiting there for them. After I took them to her room I came out and sat on the front step. I'd just add to the confusion, inside. And for some reason, even though I'm not usually squeamish, I didn't want to see them work on the kid.

I haven't chewed my fingernails since I was twelve years old and my father gave me two bucks if I'd stop. There on the that front stoop, when I'd gone through all the State Express I had, I knocked off fingernails one to ten, like I was chewing gum. It must have been an hour before the stretcher finally came out. Her head was visible above the blanket. She still looked peaceful, but now she looked almost alive. Maybe it was my imagination, but I thought I saw a little color in her face.

Danny Moore came out and leaned against the railing just above me, and I looked around and up at him.

"Got a cigarette?" I asked.

"Sure. Here."

"Is she going to make it?"

"You want kind words, or an opinion?"

"Just say."

"No. She's headed for an operating room, emergent. I was talking to the hospital, and Fish is washing up now. The bullet went through, all right, but he's a wizard if he can plug the holes."

"What did you do?"

"Kept her alive. Adrenalin directly into the heart. All the plasma the wagon carried, but she's still hemorrhaging. I sent her off because they may be able to get whole blood at the hospital."

"I'd give—"

"Sure, and what type are you? You know? I wish I could make a law that every bastard and bitch in the country had to have his blood type tattooed on his arm . . . Oh, well." He threw away his butt.

"You want to call the cops?" I asked him.

"You found her."

"Okay. I'll buzz Framboise, in a few minutes. When can they—" I stopped and started the sentence over. "Will they be able to get a statement from her? Will she recover consciousness?"

Danny Moore shook his head. "Not that I can see. If at all, not for a long while. . . . Come, buy me a drink. We both need one."

I stood. He picked up his medicine bag and started down the steps. "Sorry. I'm going back inside to work," I told him.

He looked at me narrowly. "What was she to you?"

"She was mixed up with an old friend of mine. Guy named Crawfie Foster. You treated him for a bullet wound once—something, I'm sorry to say, that was very minor. I sent him to the big box, but he got out again."

"I remember him."

"I don't know where he is, except he's somewhere in Montreal. And I'll give you odds of twenty to zero he did this. I'm going in there again to try to make sure. Then I'm going looking for him. When I'm through with him I'll call you, if you don't think it'll make you sick to come look at him. Because he'll look like a land-mine exploded under his ankles."

Danny said soberly, "I'd come, but I wouldn't work too hard on him. Call me later. I'm going back to my office and hit the lab-alky for a while. And don't forget to tell the cops about this, because otherwise I'm probably compounding a felony, or something."

Priscilla Dover had lived in a large, square room. You entered near one corner and the wall to the left contained two high, broad windows, a window-seat, a cheap chest of drawers and a straight chair. The wall opposite the door had the day bed and her desk, with chair; the wall to the right was taken up by three doors which led respectively to a closet, a bathroom and a kitchenette. The closet was about normal size and the other facilities were in rooms about the size of the closet.

The closet had a fair array of clothes, including a bulky muskrat coat she hadn't got around to storing for the summer. There were two antique suitcases shoved back behind the clothes, and hat boxes on the shelf. It took me twenty minutes to make sure there was nothing in the suitcases but old tissue paper, nothing in the hat boxes but hats, and nothing of consequence in the clothes—either in the pockets or sewn into the linings. I put another twenty minutes on the bathroom and kitchenette, looking in the obvious places; looking for something tied under the water in the toilet tank, or taped to the underside of the wash basin or sink or stove, or under the shelf-paper in the cupboards. I drew two more blanks.

That left me with the room itself, and as I went over it methodically I slowly developed the conviction I was wasting my time. She hadn't been shot to take something away from her; she'd been shot to close her mouth. Her assailant knew she had not found or written down evidence against him. Otherwise, rather than shooting, a procedure that makes noise and is likely to attract attention, he would have disposed of her silently and left himself time to tear the place apart.

I had nothing for my trouble except a drawerful of her personal letters. Most of them were in the same hand, and postmarked Winnipeg, Manitoba. I read one, and it was from her mother, a chatty old soul. I gathered Priscilla had been in Montreal for some time but came home to visit when she could raise the dough. Her mother was proud she was a success as a commercial photographer—I don't blame the kid if she didn't go into too much detail about her job with someone who wouldn't understand—and very, very proud of her ability as a skier. It seemed the kid had won trophies for downhill and slalom. I didn't see them. Maybe they were at her ski-club cabin, or maybe she'd had to hock them when Crawfie didn't pay her.

It was interesting to know about her past but it didn't get me anywhere.

I called Danny Moore again. "Got a problem. When you run across a stiff, you can make a fair guess how long he's been dead. I walked in on the kid here, and thought she'd been killed maybe an hour before I got to her. But being only wounded, I suppose it's harder to tell when it was done?"

"Depends on how fast she bled. I'd hate to guess."

"One hour? Ten hours?"

"One hour," he said, "or less. Or ten hours, or maybe even more. We might tell a little more after the operation, but I doubt it."

"Are you keeping in touch with the hospital?" I asked.

"I am."

"Easier for you to get information than for me. I'll call you. By the way, I want her in a private room, and I'm standing her tab. I expect to get somebody to reimburse me, but I'll be responsible."

"You're already down on her admission sheet."

I hung up and looked at my watch. It was too early for Framboise to be on duty, but I could probably catch him lapping his pre-dinner beer at home.

I dug in the side of the desk, hauled the phone book out by its cover, and it fell open on my knee.

Fell open at her hiding-place.

I'd found something important; something that could explain why she was shot, why Crawfie Foster pulled out of a remunerative set-up and disappeared, where he was now and what he was doing.

I couldn't see how it tied together, but I was convinced that it would.

I held another photo like the one I'd pulled from behind the desk drawer in Crawfie's old office. It was a picture of a man, hat on his head, shouldering into his coat as he stepped through an open apartment door. And this time the man was familiar.

His face was one you saw staring from the financial pages two or three times a year, as he became director of yet another corporation. He was slim, neat, grey-haired man of medium height, with level eyes and a skin as smooth and clean as a dinner place after use by a fifteen-year-old boy. He was Hamish MacFaden, vice-president and general manager of the Bank of London, one of the big Chartered banks.

It was the same apartment door as in the other picture.

I felt a stirring of an idea of what was going on. It was only a stirring, and the idea was fantastic, but I was beginning to get a crawly feeling, as though I were sinking into quicksand.

Chapter Nine

FRAMBOISE ARRIVED with a squad of boys about seven o'clock, and he grilled me while the boys went to work on the room. I told him the whole story—how I'd heard Foster was back in town, the girl had come to me to get her pay, I'd looked around Crawfie's deserted studio (I told him the janitor let me in), and the girl had told me, scared half out of her head, that she'd seen Foster again. Then I come here and find this.

The only things I missed in my recital were the two pictures. I needed to do a little more work on them, private-like.

"We'll pick up t'is guy Foster," Framboise declared.

"Have fun," I said sweetly. "He won't be easy to find. I have a hunch he's lying really low, for some reason—not working, nor appearing on the public street."

Framboise was matter-of-fact. "We got t'e routine, t'e resources, to do t'e job. Sure, be hard for you to fin' Foster. But we can check on ever'one who's move' around t'e city at end of las' month. We get 'im."

"It'll be a lot of trouble."

He shrugged. "Wort' it. It's maybe for murder we can book 'im, w'en we fin' him."

He left me to talk to his men; they all talked rapidly in French for a minute. They'd dug the spent bullet out of the mattress, but that was all they had. Framboise came back to me and said, "W'ere does t'is tie in wit' the murder of Chesterley?"

"What do you mean?"

"T'ey're bot' tied aroun' you, the two cases."

"Sometimes I work on two cases at once," I explained patiently, "like now. I hadn't even thought of any connection between the two. Now I think of it, there isn't any."

"Ah!" he said, gloating that he'd trapped me into an admission, "T'en you are working on t'e Chesterley case."

"Yeah."

"W'y?"

"Because I figured the two torpedoes who slugged me in my apartment were mixed up in Chesterley's death."

"How you figure t'at?"

"By elimination. Purely by elimination," I said, and played dumb when he asked me what else I knew about the case. After a while he got tired cat-and-mousing me, and he and his boys left.

I called Danny Moore and there was no word form the hospital about Priscilla, and then I left too. I got the Morris and U-turned it on MacKay, went up to Sherbrooke and cruised east.

I was too late to catch the day-shift at the Elephant Tavern now, and that meant I wouldn't get any dope on Crawfie from that source until tomorrow.

The Riley always had a homing instinct. It couldn't go down Sherbrooke from Guy to Peel in a straight line; it always automatically headed into a parking spot just in front of the Trafalgar. Oddly enough, I now found the Morris had quickly developed the same habits. I didn't fight the inevitable. I eased it to the curb and went into the Traf bar.

Nobody I knew was there. MacArnold was sitting at a table staring blankly at the doorway, right through me, but I didn't know him. His mother wouldn't have known him. He had two large black holes in his head where his eyes should have been, his skin was green as a chlorophyll pill, and his very hair seemed exhausted and hanging wispily off his scalp, like the paper streamers in front of a fan droop when it's turned off. He raised his glass to his mouth as I watched, and his hand was shaking so badly I expected him to knock out two or three teeth before his lips closed over the rim.

I went and sat beside him, and I'll swear he didn't know I was there until I spoke. "Hangover?" I asked.

What he was using for a voice that evening was two tones huskier than the Lachine Canal fog-horn. "Ate something that upset my stomach," he said briefly.

Alex came quietly up to the table to serve us. "Bring me a Molson," I said. "And I think my uncle, here, could use a pint of whole blood."

It was a crack, but what it reminded me of sent me back in haste to a telephone again. How could I be cracking around when the kid was probably dying on an operating table? But when I phoned Danny the news was good.

"Not out of the woods, but I was talking to Fish and he thinks she'll pull it off," he said. "The bullet didn't do as much damage as I thought at first. Her big problem was all the blood she lost, but they're pumping that back in now."

"When can I talk to her?"

"Look, flat-heels, it's more important to keep her alive than to find out who shot her. I'm in charge on this one, and I say she doesn't see anyone for three days—supposing she could talk before then, which isn't likely."

"You're the doctor," I said, a little fatuously. I didn't care how I sounded, I felt good. I liked the kid, from the little I knew about her and the few times I'd met her. I'd still have as much pleasure stoning the bastard who shot her, now that she was going to live. But it made the entire business seem a little less bloody.

I felt so good I went back into the bar and told Alex, "I'm giving this beer to my friend. I'm celebrating. Bring me a zombie. See if you can hit me with it."

"Please," MacArnold said, flushing a dull grey, "don't drink that at this table."

I looked all around the room. Unexpectedly, I saw something. "Okay. I won't," I said agreeably. "I'll be back later."

I walked over and sat down beside Elena Giotto without even being asked.

She was all alone at a small table, and must have been waiting for someone—the Traf isn't the kind of place where girls sit alone at tables in the evening, hoping. She looked up, surprised, when I sat down, and it took her a minute to remember who I was.

I tried to make a strong opening gambit. "Hello. Did you know you had a double?"

She looked at me lazily. Her eyes were very dark, and they made you want to come closer, much closer. "Yes," she said calmly.

"Oh." There didn't seem much else to say.

"I suppose you mean, do I know there is a girl in Montreal who looks very much like me? Yes, several people have told me so. They have even mistaken her for me and spoken to her. I have never seen her."

"She came to my apartment the other evening. I thought it was you."

"Mr. Teed," she smiled, "you have great presumption."

"I never do dentistry on gift horses. You come to my apartment, I invite you in. So I get your double in my place, and she behaves like a serpent's tooth. Lets in two slugger-thugs who try to knock me apart."

"Ah. I begin to get a clear picture of her personality. I hope no one ever mistakes *me* for *her*. And did they injure you?"

"No. But she did. She hit me with a bottle."

Another voice came into the conversation. It was male. It said, "Are you still feeling the effects, old man?"

Paul Hanwood was standing above us. Ten years ago I could have said he was livid with rage, but now the phrase is hackneyed. He was a dark orchid colored with rage.

"I'm still feeling lots of effects," I said politely. "I shall feel the effect of your introducing me to Elena for years, undoubtedly, years. You have only you to blame."

"I believe Elena was waiting for me," he pointed out. "No doubt you have friends you can rejoin?"

I got up, gathering my zombie off the table. "You got here too soon. If I'd finished this I'd have been with you for the evening. As it is, I still remember I'm a gentleman."

"Teed, you were never a gentleman."

I tried to think up a good reason for hitting him, but I wasn't drunk enough to think of one. I went back to Mac.

"There is a jealous man," I said.

"An old acquaintance, I think you said? Just knows your habits, that's all."

I studied MacArnold. "You can't afford to be so bitter, with a hangover like that," I decided. "I could snap my fingers in front of your face, and the noise would split your head open."

"Nah," he boasted. "I feel better." He exhibited the large beer glass he was raising. "First solid food I've been able to take all day. And see, the hand's steady."

"If you feel that much better, I have something we can work on." I hauled two photos out of my pocket. The first was the picture I'd found in Crawfie's old desk.

MacArnold held it to the light and examined it closely. "I suppose this is significant," he grunted, "but it doesn't tell me a thing."

"Recognize the guy?"

"Nope. Never saw him. He's got dressed to leave, and is proceeding out of an apartment doorway. It might be any apartment—you can't even see the number on the door."

"Now try this one." I handed him the second shot.

"Huh." He was surprised, when he'd had a good look at it. "Hamish MacFaden. Same apartment doorway." He meditated, and all I got out of him for a while was another "Huh."

"Smell anything?" I asked him.

"Sure I do. Blackmail. What is this, part of our case?"

"You mean the Chesterley killing? No, it's not that. Our friend Crawfie Foster disappeared the end of last month. I got a hunch he crawled out of the great sewer today and did a shooting—Priscilla Dover, the little photo-gal you sent to me. Those two photos are all the spoor he's left behind him."

"Where does that get you?"

"Nowhere," I admitted.

"You want to find Foster, no doubt?"

"No doubt. But I've got Framboise looking for him right now. He can turn him up faster than I can."

"And Crawfie killed the Dover kid? The bastard."

"Not quite, but he tried hard."

"Why?"

"She had this photo." I touched the shot of Hamish MacFaden. "I suppose she also knew why it was important. I wish I did."

"Got any guesses?"

"Sure. I don't know what's behind that apartment door, but it's somewhere down the line between a brothel and a dope-den. Crawfie is set up somewhere across the hall, and as people go out he trips the shutter on his little camera. A certain percentage of the guys he shoots would probably be very happy to buy back the negatives."

"Yeah," MacArnold said dreamily. He lapsed into meditation again. Talking to him was something like trying to carry on a conversation with a Great Dane drowsing in front of a fireplace.

I went on, more to hear myself reasoning than for any impression it made on him. "This must be a good racket, whatever it is. Crawfie pulled out of a set-up where he was on the gravy-train, and legitimately, to concentrate on this. The blackmail pay-off must be high, because Crawfie's been in the fly-trap once already. I understand they teach 'em to hate the idea of going back. So it's a cinch—"

"Alex!" MacArnold suddenly roared at the waiter.

Nobody had yelled that loud in the Trafalgar bar since somebody gave Murgatroyd Mitchell a hot-foot there, back in 1927. Alex came toward us like he was a yo-yo and we were holding the string.

"Alex," Mac whooped, "I want to celebrate a great idea. I want a straight double rye, and just one ice cube in it. And bring a double ginger ale for Mr. Teed."

I fixed MacArnold with my glinting eye and said very coldly: "What the hell?"

"Don't you get it?"

"No, and if it isn't good I'm calling in the A.A."

"You said there was no connection between this Foster deal and the Chesterley case. How dull can you get?"

He let me think it over while Alex brought the drinks, and while I sent him back to pour the ginger ale down the sink and mix me another zombie.

"All right," I admitted, "it's possible."

"We start with a murder on top of Mount Royal. The stiff is a partner in a gambling house. The gambling house turns out to be very high-class, patronized by the upper tax brackets. And it isn't a house. It's an apartment."

"Okay, okay, but—"

"Why was Chesterley killed? Crawfie has started pulling a blackmail gag on his clients, shooting them when they come out of the apartment and then holding them up. So he protests, naturally, because it's bad for business. And Crawfie either rubs him out or pays to have it done."

"Yeah, but why—"

"Stop interrupting me," MacArnold yapped. "Remember the set-up in that apartment house? The door of apartment fifteen was right across the corridor from sixteen. Know who's sitting behind a peep-hole in apartment fifteen, with a loaded camera?"

"Crawfie," I guessed, "you think. And let me round out your theory. Priscilla Dover somehow traced Crawfie to this hide-out, got in, copped the pic of Hamish MacFaden, and realized what the gag was. So Crawfie caught up with her a day later and tried to knock her off. Fine."

"Sure. That fits in, too."

"But there's one thing that doesn't fit in. And a theory is only good if it explains all the known facts. If one fact doesn't agree, throw out the whole thing. Explain to me why Irish Joe and his pet monkey tried to slug me the other night."

"Easy," MacArnold said, without even waiting for a swig from his glass. "Crawfie and Irish Joe are in on this together. The boy who was out in the cold was Chesterley, Irish Joe's partner in the gambling rig. Chesterley therefore gets lumped."

I couldn't think of anything to say. It looked like we might be at the end of the road in this one. The facts could all be made to fit into one pattern—a pattern curiously like the one I had put together myself, but I had failed to make the key link between the two cases.

I was getting old if I had to let MacArnold solve my cases for me.

I got up. "Okay, let's go. I'm game to try," I said.

"Try what?"

"Testing your theory. There's one obvious thing to do. We just knock on the door of number fifteen, and see if Crawfie answers."

"Oh, yeah. Are you wearing your bullet-proof vest tonight?"

"For Crawfie I wouldn't wear mosquito netting."

"He wouldn't be alone in there, not in a racket like this. He'd have about six mugs with him. Anyway you know you'd never get through his door without a special knock."

"Maybe we can't prove your theory," I said patiently, "but we can see if it's easy to disprove. We knock, and if nothing happens or if we get warned off, maybe Crawfie is in there. If somebody perfectly innocent lives in the place, we see them and then come back here and start on another theory."

A small boy with a pill-box cap through the bar chanting in a dim voice, "Mr. Smerth! Mr. Smertherlamb! Mr. Teed!"

I was glad my name wasn't Sutherland. There wasn't much he could do to Teed. I called him over and he said I was wanted on the phone. I went.

"Greetings," a solid male voice said.

"Hyah. Who?"

"Montgomery. Anything happen last night?"

"No. MacArnold and I nearly got killed early this morning, though. Where are you?"

"At the Alamo again. Bored as hell."

"Come around here and meet us. I wouldn't be sure, but I think things may happen."

"Interesting?"

"Sure. You might even be in on the kill."

Afterward he said I was a prophet. He didn't know I didn't know, when I said it, what kill.

Chapter Ten

One thing you can say about good ol' Teed, good ol' Teed knows his limishashionsh. Limi—knows his capashity. Teed knows when he's drunk, and it's no sense getting drunker.

So while we waited for Montgomery, I didn't have a third zombie.

Montgomery came, and even in my state I could recognize that beaded, misty look about his eyes that meant he'd been pouring them down faster than they would spread out. We got out of the Trafalgar and walked a short distance in the open air, and it did all of us at least a slight bit of good.

The tired trio of MacArnold, Montgomery and Teed came to the entry of the apartment building that housed the gambling spot. MacArnold was still a summery shade of green, Montgomery was not in good shape to discuss his inheritance with a wealthy maiden aunt, and Teed was dreaming of a white Christmas—I could have used some of the snow to wash my face and sober me up.

"Wait," I said importantly, "I have got to decide what we are going to do."

"See who lives in apartment fifteen," MacArnold reminded me.

"Yes, but let's not miss any golden opportunities. You and I can't go back into the gambling den, but our friend Montgomery can."

"Sure," said Montgomery.

I narrowed my eyes and tried to look at him narrowly. "In your condition, you'll lose money," I decided.

Montgomery made a great play of dragging out his wallet and counting the folding money. "Anything up to fifty bucks I don't mind," he said.

"Fifty bucks wouldn't keep you in the place ten minutes." I turned to MacArnold. "You still got expense money? Give him a century. It's all for the good of the story."

I held out my hand. MacArnold was too weak to argue. He counted out a hundred in twenties and tens, into my palm. I put it in my pocket and gave Montgomery ten of the little red chips I'd picked up the night before. "They're legal tender inside," I told him. "Buy a few from the table man to allay suspicion, and then use 'em."

I felt a lot better.

"You go up first," I instructed Montgomery. "Tell the watch-dog at number sixteen that Louie Two sent you. Once you're inside, watch for a little guy masked by bandages and a heavy-handed ape with a rough jaw. Report on what they do. Don't get in trouble."

He was wafted upward in the elevator. We gave him ten minutes to get inside number sixteen, and then called the cage back and went up to the eighth floor. While we were rising MacArnold said, "You better handle this. I think I'm a little slowed up tonight. I only just realized what happened to my hundred bucks."

The doors slapped back for the eighth floor. MacArnold took a deep breath. "Let's go."

"I got something to do first."

I went over and stood in front of the door to sixteen. Then I took out of my pocket the two photos I'd picked up, the one from Crawfie's desk and the second where Priscilla had hidden it. I studied them and looked at the door. MacArnold came up and watched over my shoulder.

MacArnold studied the pics too. He looked at the door. "Guess where those were taken," he grunted.

"See this?" I pointed. On both photos a scar showed

about halfway up the left side of the door frame, raw against the dark wood. And on both photos there was an irregularity at the end of the top member of the frame, where the wood hadn't been properly squared.

These marks showed clearly, if you needed convincing, that both pics had been taken from the same spot. And they corresponded exactly to marks on the door frame of apartment sixteen.

"We're onto something, all right," I declared. "Where would you say these were taken from?"

MacArnold looked over his shoulder. His back was nearly touching the door of number fifteen. "From right here. Or rather from somewhere just behind this door."

"Something bothers me. How could he get enough light to take these, in this dim hallway, without using a flash that would reveal what he was doing?"

MacArnold explained in self-satisfied tones. "You may bow to my superior technical knowledge, lug. He'd use an infra-red flash and a film sensitive to infra-red light. There's no visible flash when the bulb goes off, but it gets the picture all the same."

That might have been the explanation, or there might be another one. I wasn't willing to trust Mac a hundred per cent. But one thing was certain: even though the apartment number was not visible in the pictures, they were shots of people coming through the doorway of sixteen. They were taken from straight across the hall, meaning from or near apartment fifteen. And even though the whole thing was MacArnold's idea, and made me look an awful lot dumber than I like to think I am, it seemed he was right on the essentials.

Crawfie, always ready for a crooked deal that paid enough, had teamed with Irish Joe in a scheme to milk the patrons of the gambling spot. Crawfie was to set up in fifteen and snap them one by one as they emerged. Probably Irish Joe had originated the idea, and Chesterley had objected—which got him nothing but a funeral he had to pay for himself.

Now all we had to do was check on the set-up. We had to place Crawfie in number fifteen. We had to see Hamish MacFaden, or someone else if he wouldn't talk, and get an admission that blackmail had been going on. And we had to scare Irish Joe into admitting his part in the plan and in the death of Chesterley on Mount Royal.

Obviously, the first step was to knock on the door of fifteen. I wished I was soberer. I didn't feel like investigating the disappearance of cookies from a cookie jar, at that moment.

"Brace up," MacArnold said sympathetically.

I looked at him. He was about the color of a field of unripe alfalfa. I said sourly, "You can do it if you want to."

"Not me. I'm just the idea man on this team. You do the leg work."

"And run the risks."

I found a bell and punched it. Behind us came the whirr of the self-service elevator. There was only one chance in ten it was coming to this floor, but I didn't especially want the door of sixteen to open while we were in the corridor. I paused. When the fifteen bell was answered I grabbed MacArnold by the jacket and levered us both inside without even waiting to see who had come to the door for us. As soon as we were in I caught the bottom panel with the back of my heel and slammed it behind us. I didn't know what we were into, but we were in.

The character whose apartment we had invaded stood with eyebrows raised and mouth open about one-half inch. He was surprised, but the general aspect of him led me to believe he might be as angry as surprised.

He was a tall man, carefully groomed, with slick black hair and a distinctive family-type nose you could likely trace in portraits back to the First Crusade. He was wearing evening clothes, and the only possible mark of distinction in evening clothes—the white bow-tie—had been carefully hand tied.

His name was Paul Hanwood.

"Evening," I said pleasantly. "I was looking for a crap game. Louie Two sent me here. Didn't expect to find you, Paul."

"I live here," he told me coldly.

"You run a crap game?"

"The crap game is across the hall. Any time you want to leave and go there is all right with me."

MacArnold had been pawing around, "Nope," he broke in, "It's impossible."

"What the devil do you think you're doing?" Paul snapped.

"This door," Mac said, slapping it with a resounding crash, "is real solid oak. Moreover, the panels don't lift out. Nobody hid behind here taking pictures."

"Who would want to?"

"Leave him alone," I advised Hanwood. "He's interested in doors tonight. He thinks he's a termite."

"Ha, ha," Paul said, deadpan. "Well, sorry I can't invite you in, I'm just going out. If you're through prowling—"

"Prowling?" I used my injured innocence tone.

"Let's not play make-believe. You boys are looking for the crap game as much as I'm looking for a ruptured liver. I don't know what you want, nor how you found out I live here, but you seem interested in viewing my premises, and looking for concealed cameras. Well, you've seen all I care to show you. Okay, out."

"May I tell you a little story?" I asked.

"No stories."

"This is for free. The last time we met, in the Trafalgar, I wasn't drunk enough to think up a reason for socking you. I haven't thought up a reason, but tonight I'm too drunk to need one."

It was probably the most telegraphed punch since Marconi first sent words by wire. He just stood there with a foolish look on his face and waited for it. I hit him square in the chest. I wasn't getting soft; I really meant to clip his chin. I was just a lot drunker than I thought. He went down anyway.

And as he went down a gun roared behind me, wood splintered and a bullet whistled past my head. I dropped to my hands and knees. It seemed Hanwood had pals somewhere who were sneaking up behind me.

The gun roared a second time, but I didn't hear any bullet. I shook my head and it cleared a little, after the shock. I wasn't going to be able to think fast, but maybe I'd be able to think.

Hanwood was lying on his back, frozen with fear. I guess he'd heard the bullet bang past him too. Something tapped me on the ankle, and I looked around. I'd forgotten MacArnold. He had joined us on the floor.

"I hear sirens," he said.

"It will just be a stray ambulance cruising down Sherbrooke. No cops in the world answer a shooting that fast."

MacArnold cocked his head to one side. "I hear a whole posse of sirens," he insisted. And he was right. I could hear them too.

"I think it might be safe to leave," I suggested.

I ambled to the door on my hands and knees and opened it a crack. Everything was very quiet in the corridor. The door of number sixteen was closed. There was nothing unusual around at all, except a body stretched flat on the floor just in front of my nose.

The body was lying in that silly, crumpled still position that makes you know when you see a body. It was a man, dressed in a neat dark business suit with some evidence of blood beginning to spread out from the centre of the back. He had fallen over on his face and his hat had rolled off his head.

I threw the door wide open and got to my feet. I ventured into the corridor. All was silent, and nobody took a pot-shot at me. "Come in," I called to MacArnold. "I think the cops are coming, and I know we're leaving."

He stuck his nose out the door. I went to the side of the corridor and shoved the button for the elevator. Then I couldn't restrain my curiosity any longer, and while the elevator ground up to the eighth floor I went back to the body and lifted his shoulder gently, just to see who he was.

I'd never met the gentleman, but I can't say his face was totally unfamiliar. It was a face I was carrying around in my pocket; not Hamish MacFaden, but the anonymous character in the photo from Crawfie's desk.

The elevator arrived then. I got in, and MacArnold dashed out of Paul Hanwood's apartment and into the cage, running with a weaving motion of his shoulders as though trying to avoid a firing squad. He wasn't green any more, either; fear had bleached him laundry-white.

We rode down in silence. The doors opened at the lobby floor, and there was Framboise, waiting with hands on hips.

"*Allo*," he grunted. "W'ats up?"

"You tell me."

"We jus' get a phone call. Someone says a murder 'as

been committed 'ere."

"Oh? Where?"

"On t'e heighth floor."

"Wouldn't know anything about it," I said calmly. "We just came down from seeing some dear old friends on the tenth. Come on, Mac."

I shouldered past him and weaved through six of his squad that stood about the foyer. MacArnold came too.

"I'll remember you were 'ere!" Framboise bawled after us, but I ignored that.

We got to the sidewalk. "Well goodbye," I told MacArnold. "Each for himself. When Framboise finds out from Paul Hanwood that we were on the eighth, he'll be after us. Let's git, if we want to stay free."

MacArnold headed west at a stiff-legged lope. I didn't even try to keep up appearances. I ran. I ran east.

I hadn't gone more than a few pounding steps when a car door at the curb sprang open just beside me. A husky feminine voice said, "Get in."

Feminine voice.

That was enough for me, and I got in, and it was Elena Giotto. She was driving a beautiful cream-colored Jaguar convertible. I relaxed on red leather upholstery and she pulled away from the curb, letting out the clutch to a surge of pure mechanical power that jerked my head back against the seat. It was nice to be riding in a trigger-happy car again.

Elena laughed richly. "I saw the police come in. And then you came out, and started running. I judged you would wish to be elsewhere."

"Very elsewhere," I said.

"We will go for a long drive."

"That suits me fine."

I closed my eyes and enjoyed the swift motion of the car. A very unpleasant thing was happening. I was beginning to sober up, and my head was aching more than slightly, and if I didn't get a drink soon I probably wouldn't be able to drink for two days.

"Maybe a nice bar would be better than a long drive."

"We will combine the two. A roadhouse."

"What will Paul say?"

She shrugged. "It's all right. He won't know."

"Sure?"

"Well, he can't come after us. This is his car."

Chapter Eleven

Some people make you remember things; some people make you forget. I looked sideways at Elena Giotto, driving the car with a beautiful feeling for the task, a little frown of concentration on her smooth face, a free grace in the movement of her arms at the wheel. Elena made me forget. She made me forget any of the women who had ever been important to me, and the few who were currently important.

Her accent was foreign, her name made her Italian, but her profile was straight from Ancient Greece. She had a very straight, well-turned nose, high and accented angles of the cheek-bones; she wore her chin thrust firmly, tantalizingly forward, daring the world to touch her.

And here was one small, detached clod who wouldn't resist the impulse to touch her much longer.

We went straight east on Sherbrooke Street, the Jaguar covering miles in no time at all. At Lafontaine Park she turned down toward the river, stopped while I paid the bridge toll, and then spun across the long, arching Jacques Cartier Bridge. Then we went through Longueuil, turned east on a road that ran parallel to the St. Lawrence, and finally came to a halt in the broad parking area before a long, low roadhouse.

I had opened my door and was halfway out of the car before we realized the place was dark and deserted. "Oh," she said in annoyance. "I thought it funny their neon sign was not burning. I thought perhaps it had just gone out. But look, they are not extending hospitality here tonight."

"Who cares?" I got back in the car and slammed the door. I fished out the State Express and lit two and gave her one. "Leave us relax for a moment," I suggested. "Later, we can hunt up another one. Unless this is a Catholic holiday, and they're all closed. That I could stand too."

"Oh?"

"There are things I like to do more than drink."

She turned a rather stony face toward me. "I think I know what you mean, and—"

"Talk, for instance. I think your voice is lovely. I want to listen to you talk."

"Well, let us be clear about things. Remember, we—"

"We've scarcely met, you aren't the kind of girl who picks up men and lets them kiss her, sure, I know. Who are you, Elena?"

"A girl from Italy. In Canada only for a few months."

"How did you happen to come here? Relatives?"

"No. I—wanted to come. It was arranged."

I thought about some things I knew, matters that weren't public knowledge but that I had certain reasons for knowing, because of a little work I'd helped a Government department do. They were things I didn't like to connect with her. So the only thing to do was be straight with it, and not let it hammer around in my brain. I asked her, "Did you come legally?"

She shrugged. I was wondering about her, but I had to admit she shrugged beautifully. "I am very stupid about such things. Legally? I don't know. It was all arranged. I had certain papers which were perfectly in order."

"I don't think you're stupid at all. I think you know more than you're saying."

The tip of her cigarette glowed fiercely in the darkness, and she puffed a white curtain of smoke across the windshield. "Of course," she said slowly, "of course I know more than that. What are you? An Immigration agent?"

"No. Just a guy."

"Have you seen Italy recently? Go see Italy sometime. Dress in ragged clothes and go walking around the parts of the wrecked cities where most of the people must live. Try to find work. Try to buy food!"

"Maybe I don't blame you," I said. "I'm not sure. But you may land yourself in the middle of an awfully dirty mess."

"Paul says not."

"He brought you over?"

"He met me last summer, while he was travelling in Italy. He arranged for my emigration to Canada. And mark, it was perhaps quite legal. I honestly am not sure."

"Then why act so guilty about it?"

"I came under false pretences. Paul thought I came because I loved him, but I came because I wanted good food again, and new clothes, and—" Her voice broke, and she was crying.

I waited it out, with another cigarette, having done the big brother act by providing my clean show-handkerchief to be wetted down.

Her voice was shaky when she went on. "When I say it, even to myself, it sounds mercenary and cheap. But one can resist an overpowering temptation only so long. And Italy, without money—"

"We're all human," I said profoundly. In times of stress we are all corny, too, I noted mentally, listening to myself.

"Women have sold themselves for much less. I have played fair with Paul, been his girl since I came here. I've made a bargain, I feel, and I won't go back on that."

"So what are you doing now?" I realized as soon as I said it that the suggestion was hardly in my best interests, but I wanted her honestly or not at all. It would splinter my heart, but I'd get right out and walk home if she was about to be dishonest with herself. Or if she didn't have the capacity to stick to something she'd decided was square.

What happened was what I might have expected. It proved she was winning a fight with herself, but it also left Teed as just the old shoe dragging along behind the honeymoon car.

She turned on the car lights and the ignition and turned over the engine. "We had better look for that open roadhouse we were going to find."

"Or would you sooner go home?"

She turned the car back onto the road with a vicious jerk of the wheels, pointing it toward Montreal. "An excellent idea," she said grimly.

It took us half an hour to get back to the heart of the city, but the total conversation amounted to less than a dozen words. We cruised Sherbrooke West and passed the apartment building where Paul Hanwood and the crap game lived.

"Where are you going?" I asked her.

"I was waiting to pick up Paul, when I called to you. I'll go back later and get him, if he's still there. First I shall take you home."

"It's not necessary."

"I do not expect you want to be let out of the car at Paul's door. Perhaps the police are still there. Come, tell me where you live. Paul said it was on Cote des Neiges."

She turned up the hill and the Jaguar climbed effortlessly toward Westmount Boulevard. "That building," I said when she'd gone far enough, and she stopped at the curb.

I got out of the convertible and hesitated before closing the door. "You can come up, if you want, and phone Paul. It would be simpler than going back and hammering on his door."

She shook her head, looking straight ahead of her, not meeting my eye.

"Believe me, I don't mean to start anything."

Then she did look at me, soberly, with some sort of question in her gaze. That went on for a few seconds before she slid easily across the car seat and got out of the car on my side. We walked wordlessly across the sidewalk and into my building, down the corridor and into the elevator. We went up to my floor.

We stepped out of the cage. My apartment is at the back of the building, at the end of the long hallway on that floor. There was a man standing at my door, but we had to walk half the distance toward him before I knew who it was.

Paul Hanwood had been waiting for us.

"Good evening," he said. I didn't like the way he said it. I didn't like what he did next, either; he brought his hand out of his topcoat pocket, with a very capable looking automatic pistol folded in his fingers.

"I was waiting to ask you if you knew what had happened to Elena," he purred. "I see I don't have to ask."

Elena was petrified. She stopped with a jerk and stood swaying, her lips moving nervously and her red tongue flicking over them. I just kept on walking toward Paul Hanwood.

"Okay, Scarface Algernon," I said softly. "Never mind the melodrama. Put it away and take your girl home."

He went back one step to keep me a safe distance from him and the gun. "We'll talk for a minute first," he said. "I'd like a little information on where you've been, and what you've been doing—in my car."

I kept coming.

"You can stop right there," he blurted. You're close enough"

I didn't say anything. I kept coming. I knew he wouldn't be fool enough to shoot—he wasn't crazy mad, and he was too cool a bastard to want to hang himself.

I didn't think he would do anything. I was wrong.

I got nearly close enough to touch him, and I would have had my arms quickly on his and the gun pinned to his side, but he moved like a dog snapping at flies. The blue gun flashed up and came down once, twice, on my arm and then on my shoulder. I staggered back a half-step and he let me have the gun hard, the flat of the gun to the side of my head.

It wasn't much worse than being hit on the side of the head by a snowball, if you can imagine a snowball packed by a hydraulic ram and thrown by an oversize gorilla with a good pitching arm. I nearly went down for ten or twelve. My legs felt strong as if they were made of wet newspaper, and the hall rocked slowly around me as I sagged. I pulled myself back just before my knuckles touched the floor.

He stepped to me and took me by the elbow. "We'll finish this inside, in private," he snarled. He loved seeing me groggy. "Open up," he ordered.

I shook my head. Nothing had broken loose inside, and when I looked at the floor I was happy to see neither of my ears had fallen off. I let Hanwood guide me forward and plant me in front of my door, and I took my time fumbling in my pocket for my keys. I gave myself long enough to coordinate my mind and muscles again.

I got out my keys and unlocked the door. I was careful to keep a glazed look in my eyes, but behind that I was nearly back to normal. I stepped back, and I could feel the muzzle of the automatic punch the right side of my back. I thought Paul had been holding the thing in his right hand, but I wanted to be really sure.

To excuse myself for moving back I said, sluggishly and thickly, "Ladies first. Elena c'n go in."

He prodded with his gun. "Go ahead. She'll follow."

I stepped through the door and went two steps on into

the entry. Hanwood was right behind, and when I stopped suddenly his gun bumped me again. Then I pulled the job on him, and it was over faster than I can tell it.

It was a little stunt we learned very early in Commando training. We used to practise it there with loaded guns, just to give everybody confidence. It always worked; we didn't lose a single man. It has to be done just so, but if you know how, you're safe as a ball player sitting on the first base sack.

If a man has a gun on your back, and if you know which hand he's holding the gun in, and if the gun is actually touching your back—twist, zip, boom, splat.

The twist was as I suddenly threw myself around at him, the zip was the edge of my hand slashing simultaneously down on his gun-wrist, the boom was the bullet from the deflected gun hitting the wall a good foot away from me, and the splat was my other hand homing to the point of his jaw to put him to sleep.

It was all over in seconds, but I felt good when it was over, like you feel good the instant after you've pulled the rip-cord and the parachute slices past your ears and starts to fill up with wind.

The whole thing is based on reaction times; it's impossible for the most trigger-happy guy in the world to flex his finger in time to weight you down with lead, once you start to move. I was surprised at Paul for being so dumb. Strictly an amateur. All the pro boys are onto the gag now, and keep a good three feet between the gun and the target.

I surveyed the situation, and Elena was somewhere in the hall out of sight. I drew off and kicked Hanwood in the ribs, hard enough to break a few. That was for the love-pat from his gun. It had my head still ringing, and I was annoyed with him. I wasn't too tough on him, either. I could have kicked him in the face. This rib job would just mean a sore chest and a few dozen yards of adhesive tape. And it would keep him from being very active at night for a while, if he slept with Elena.

Elena was the next problem. I went out into the hall and she was standing rigidly just where we left her, her eyes glazed and her mouth a bit ajar. I don't know to this day whether I did it from anger and frustration, or from sympathy, but I gave her one sharp slap across the cheek and it brought her out of the daze. She caught her breath with a gasp and stared at me.

"Nobody's dead. Nobody's even bleeding," I said harshly. "Go inside."

I was following her in, when the apartment door next to mine opened a wide crack, and a disembodied head hung itself out into the hall, like a large edam cheese swinging on the end of a string. It was an old head, not very well-preserved and more dishevelled than I cared to see in my apartment building.

"Ah, Mrs. MacEchran. That was the name on her door tag, though I'd never seen her before in my five years in the building. I presumed she was fed intravenously by a pipeline from some nearby hospital.

"The noise," I said soothingly. "I'm so sorry. It must have startled you."

She goggled at me. Her eyes goggled and her mouth goggled. She didn't say a word. One hand poked out beneath the head. Palm up. In the palm was a slightly scarred bullet.

I thought of telling her I'd had an inconvenient accident while cleaning my gun, causing the bullet to appear though her wall, and then I realized detailed explanations would be useless. She looked like an unkempt witch. She had enough red hair for eagles to nest in, and a nose of a type seldom seen much higher up the evolutionary scale than orangutans.

And, for a witch, she didn't look smart enough to even set water on fire. I went up to her and gently relieved her of the bullet. "Thank you so much," I said. "I'll put it back in the gun and use it again."

I left her there with the useless part of her anatomy protruding into the hall and went back to the world of reality.

Elena was working on Paul. She had dragged him to the side of the entry and sat him up against the wall, and she was carrying on with the traditional wrist-chafing, which doesn't usually do more for an unconscious man than warm his hands.

The automatic was lying on the floor and I picked it up and put it in my pocket. I went out to the kitchen and let the water run until it was cold. Then I drew a glassful and came back and threw it in Hanwood's face.

While he was untangling his upper eyelashes from his lowers, I watched Elena. She was unhappy, but not too upset. "He sure brought it on himself," I told her.

"Yes."

"I can't quite persuade myself that you owe anything to a guy who acts this silly."

She looked at me. She was considering it.

"If you ever decide you've worked off all your obligations, come see me. We'll have things to discuss."

Hanwood groaned.

"Ah, Junior," I said. "Before I ask you to leave, I want to make sure of a few things. Why are you living across the hall from that high-class crap joint?"

He gasped a little and made like he wasn't able to get his breath and talk. I let that go on for a minute, but I knew he was pretty fully conscious.

"Algernon!" I tapped him lightly on the cheek. "Come,

come, we must converse. Or should I send Elena away, and we can have another dance together?"

He glowered.

"Why across the hall?"

"I moved in before they did," he said bitterly. "That used to be a perfectly proper building. I don't know anything about the place, except drunks trying to get in there sometimes knock on my door by mistake."

"When did you first meet Crawfie Foster?"

"Who's he?"

"A photographer."

"I don't know any photographers."

I lifted my hand to him. "Yeah, you say."

He cringed and said rapidly, "I don't know anybody named Foster."

I grunted. I got him under the shoulders and set him up on his feet; he grimaced with pain from his caved-in ribs.

"Okay. Good night," I said.

Elena led him away and I closed the door after them.

Chapter Twelve

THE EVENTS OF THE DAY had upset me. I was in a state, in fact, to apply the train treatment.

When you're sitting in your compartment, bouncing along a roadbed, rough as all roadbeds are, wondering how you will manage to get a good night's sleep, follow my recipe. Take a bottle of good rye from your suitcase—no excuses now; if you travel without a good bottle you have no business travelling. Carefully measure four ounces into a paper cup of suitable size, add water to taste, drink it quickly, and lie down. If you aren't asleep in fifteen minutes, repeat the dose. After that, the engineer can take the locomotive off the tracks and try to climb trees, and you won't feel it.

I followed the prescription implicitly, except that I substituted glassware for the paper cups. I came into my bedroom with the initial dose in my right hand and the emergency portion in my left, undressed, sat on the bed, and took my medicine.

It had been a bad day.

From the time I tip-toed into Priscilla's room and found her shot until I'd knocked the gun from Hanwood's hand, all my ductless glands had been taxed to the capacity of their blind being. I was now emotionally sucked dry.

For a while things had looked good. Priscilla had come through surgery and MacArnold had stumbled on what might be the solution to both the cases I was working on. After that, though, things fell apart.

To prove MacArnold's theory it had to be shown that Foster lived across the hall from the gamblers and had some sort of trick set-up for imaging the departing suckers. It had to be shown that blackmail was being committed. It had to be shown that Irish Joe was in cahoots with Crawfie. I could work on the second and third items in this string, but the first seemed to be a blind herring. Crawfie didn't live in apartment fifteen, unless he was Hanwood's boy friend, which I doubted, and you can't shoot pictures through solid oak. Unless there was some way around that one, MacArnold was dead wrong, and I still had two unsolved problems on my hands instead of one case figured out and just waiting for proof.

But no. It was all one case. Item one, the pictures I'd found were definitely connected with Crawfie Foster, and just as definitely they were shots of the doorway of the gambling apartment.

Item two, the little guy who was shot in front of the gamblers' door was the little guy Crawfie had snapped.

But what was his connection with the case, why had he been killed, and who had shot him? Had he been just coming away from the crap game when he was shot? Had he been bumped by someone from inside the apartment, or had the killer been waiting for him in the hall?

Now, true, I had just one case. But it had three separate angles—the Chesterley murder, the disappearance of Crawfie Foster, and the sudden death of the little man—instead of the two earlier problems.

Verily, life was not easy.

Priscilla's shooting was another thing entirely, closely enough linked with Crawfie's hiding-out to be called part of the same problem. And it made me sick at my stomach to think of the poor kid lying there asleep, waking to the sight of a man with a gun and hear a bullet spit at her chest. A lot of things Crawfie had done made me sick, and if this was his baby, and I found him, Framboise would never see him alive.

I didn't like to think about that. I didn't like the senseless, seemingly purposeless slaying of the little man. I didn't like anything about the case. To add to all that, I was slowly going crazy about Elena and knowing all the time, trying to beat it through my stupid skull, she wasn't worth it. I didn't like her attitude. I didn't like Hanwood's attitude, either, but I'd taken steps tonight to change that.

I raised the second potion to my lips and downed it. Tonight, if he wanted to, the engineer could unhitch his engine and then come back and start playing bull-in-the-pasture with my car, and I wouldn't care.

I slept until about eight in the morning. I woke with a slight buzzing in my ears and a vague, detached feeling of being slightly doped, but I was rested and it was a beautiful day. I took off my pyjama coat and found the pants and put them on. I wandered barefoot through my well-rugged living room, threw open the French doors at the far end, and stepped onto my terrace. It was a beautiful day.

The sun was halfway up on its journey to the top of the misty, cloudless blue sky. Far away before me, haze softened the rolling tops of the blue hills across the border in the States. Nearer, the flat plain of the Laurentian lowlands was green. Self-important little boats pushed their way up the river toward the Lachine Canal. And still nearer, all beneath me, was the city I love.

Montreal is not the Paris of America, nor the New Orleans of the North, nor the Manhattan of Canada, though she had been called all those things. She is her own city, a city on an island climbing two mountains, a city cleaved down the middle by a line dividing English and French, a city with verve and yet much dignity, a good place to live and—sometimes an easy place to die.

Which brought my mind right back to the previous

night, and to my futile thoughts about the death of Chesterley, the attack on Priscilla, and the shooting of the little man.

I looked downhill toward the river, down through the mixture of old-walled dwellings with many green trees that is the picture of Montreal in spring or summer. I looked down at the old financial district—the massive height of the Royal Bank building, the smaller Aldred skyscraper, the twin towers of old Notre Dame church. I decided the next thing to do was go down there.

My terrace was bounded at the left by a waist-high masonry wall separating it from the terrace of the next apartment. From next door, I heard just then the rattle of French doors being opened. I looked back, and through the glass I could see Mrs. MacEchran's cobwebby old red wig threshing from side to side in effort as she clawed her way into the sunlight. Then the doors popped open and she was expelled onto her terrace like an old bone coughed out by a dog.

She was wearing a rust-colored wrapper that was older than her hair. A number of moths had died of over-indulgence after working on it. She had old cloth slippers that a ragpicker wouldn't have fished out of a garbage can, and there was a line of dirt around her skinny old ankles just above them. She was so much like a pile of offal I was afraid of spontaneous combustion when the sunlight hit her.

She hadn't intended to come right onto the terrace and retreated back to the edge of her French door. "Nudity!" she screamed at me, "Nakedness! This is supposed to be a respectable neighborhood. For shame! I'll report you to the police."

I hitched up my pyjama pants with one hand and waved to her with the other. "Beautiful morning," I said cordially.

She retreated, nose high, and slammed the door with a clatter. Then she opened it again a crack. "And I've told the manager," she shrilled. "I've told him how you tried to shoot me."

Slam again, and this time she was gone.

Ah, yes, lovely morning.

I went inside and to the kitchen. I got out a bottle of beer, heated up a frying pan and poured about two tablespoons of the beer in it. I broke three eggs into the pan, scrambled them, seasoned them with salt and pepper and lots of tarragon, and scraped the makings of a wonderful breakfast out onto a plate.

And somebody banged at my front door.

To hell with them. I ate the eggs.

After I'd rinsed off the plate and finished a glass of milk, and got the coffee cooking, the banging was still going on. I went to the front door and called, "Who is it?"

"Lila!"

I rubbed the top of my head. I said, "I'll count to ten, and if you aren't gone I'll come out there and break both your arms."

"I want to explain."

"You want your arms broke?"

"I'll take the chance, if you let me talk first."

"Wait a minute."

I went to the hall closet and pulled out my shoulder holster with the automatic in it. I checked the automatic to make sure it was full of lead, and took off the safety. With the holster buckled over my bare chest I went back to the door and opened it on the safety chain. It was Lila, all right.

"Stand aside," I told her. "I want to be sure the hall's clear." She got out of my line of sight and I convinced myself nobody big enough to be troublesome was in the corridor.

Then I let her in, closed the door, put the chain back on, then the snap-lock, and I turned the key on the night latch and took it out. I stuffed it in the band of my pyjamas.

Lila gazed at me. "Mmmm. Manly chest!" She reached out and ran a smooth fingertip down my ribs. Her fingernail tickled.

Feelings that are natural to any grown man at certain times began to tingle in my blood. After all, she was a beautiful girl. She looked remarkably like Elena—even if she did have a slightly different character. And after my frustrating evening, a girl who looked like Elena ran a certain risk coming here.

She'd attacked me. She couldn't complain very much if I attacked . . .

Nuh-uh, I thought. Remember Sampson, and what Delilah did to him?

"Leave the chest alone," I said harshly. "It's all right. But that's more than I can say for my head, where you socked me."

"Oh, that!" she said scornfully.

Her tone got me mad enough I didn't have to worry about yielding to her charms. "Yes, that!" I yelled. "I don't have a head made of rock, like your friend with the indigo jaw, Irish Joe, or whoever he is. When you break a bottle on my head it affects me."

"You threw a chair at me first."

"I was pretty careless. I missed you."

"Look, honest. I didn't know the lugs were going to beat you up. They gave me ten bucks to get them into your apartment. They said they just wanted to talk to you and warn you against something."

"Warn me against what?"

"They didn't say."

"Okay, so they start to beat me up. Just as I'm mopping the floor with them, you slug me. Got any good reasons why

I shouldn't slug you back right now?"

"Lots, but we'll get to those later. Look, I'm sorry. I was scared. All I could think of was you'd finish them off, and then probably beat me up, and turn all three of us over to the cops."

"Why are you scared of the cops?"

"I'm not, usually. But I doubt it would be a good idea to be picked up in company with those two."

"So why were you working for them?"

"I told you. I didn't know they were sluggers. I didn't realize how bad they were until they started working you over."

"Where did you meet them?"

"Where I work. I'm a night-club photo girl. I ran into them often in the Crystal Ball."

"Who do you work for?"

"I don't work now. Last month I worked for Foster."

"You know Priscilla Dover?"

"Sure I do. I didn't come here to enquire about your health. I heard Priscilla had been shot—her landlady told me when I phoned there this morning. I called the hospital and they wouldn't tell me anything much, except that you were listed as her next-of-kin or something. Imagine my surprise."

"Yeah," I said bitterly.

"So how is Priscilla?"

"I'll find out. Because I want to know myself, not for you."

I got Danny Moore on the phone. Priscilla had had a pretty poor night, because they didn't dare strain her heart with too much pain-killer, but she was still improving. She wasn't in condition to talk to anyone, but she'd be all right. I gave Lila the news.

"Poor kid. Who shot her?"

"One gets you ten it was Crawfie Foster, but I sure can't prove it right now. I can't even find him."

"A lot of people would like to find him. He owes me a month's wages, so I'd be very happy to see him."

"If I find him, I'll tell you."

"Thanks. I'll split with you on what I get out of him."

"Forget it. I'm not interested in making dough on this one. I just want to wring Foster's neck."

"Because you think he shot Priscilla?"

"Yep, mainly."

"You're not too bad a guy, are you?" She grinned an impish grin. She reminded me a lot of Elena, the few times Elena wasn't in a tragic mood. Lila was not as finely-groomed as Elena, and the planes of her face were not classic, but she had more life than Elena. More sparkle. And the same figure.

I thought for a minute of the picture Lila had presented with her dress unbuttoned. I noticed she was wearing a zippered dress. I turned those thoughts over in my mind for a little while and decided it might be a good idea for me to go get into a cold shower right away.

Lila said, with a teasing grin, "There was another reason why I came around. I was afraid the demonstration the other night maybe wasn't convincing."

I swallowed hard. "Demonstration?"

"About the foam rubber," she said. "Remember?" Her hand travelled slowly up to the neck of her dress. She unzipped.

It was a way too late for the shower.

"See?" she said proudly, and she could be proud.

This time there was no possibility of doubt. Because there was no brassiere.

A few minutes later she said, "Well, my golly! You might take off that old gun belt!"

Chapter Thirteen

I LIKE THE OLD DOWNTOWN part of Montreal, the old geegawed stone buildings that have been sitting there getting sootier since the city was founded, the narrow one-way streets, the stately dark-grey halls of banking and finance.

And I found, this morning, that I also liked the way the little Morris behaved in this part of town. Sometimes it had been so much trouble wheeling Riley through these streets, I'd left him behind and walked. Now the Morris puttered along, in and around irritated stalled taxis, under the running-boards of high trucks, skipping away from traffic lights with two wheels on the road and two in the gutter.

I parked on Notre Dame Street at the back door of the Bank of London—it fronts on St. James—got out, and walked leisurely across the sidewalk. Before I made the bank, a paper stand stopped me. Copies of the *Clarion* were plastered all over the stand, and the headlines were attracting customers as if they were the announcement of a new war.

FINANCIER MURDERED IN LOCAL GAMBLING DEN, the black line across the top of the paper shouted. I bought one and looked around for a place to read it. Across the street was a tavern.

I went in and ordered a quart of Molson, and sipped. The tavern was curious enough to get some of my attention before I settled down to the *Clarion*; it was a small, quiet tavern, ordinary in every respect but one—it was fronted by a large, ornate stained-glass window. The pictures of the window apparently depicted stages in the brewing of beer, but that didn't make any difference. One still got the rather eerie feeling of sitting drinking in a church. The sun came through the window and dropped a patch of crimson on my hand, holding the glass. It was only the crimson from a brewer's jacket but it was the same shade as the patch of St. Peter's robe that used to fall on my hand in the middle of the sermon, at the church I went to with mother years ago. I felt guilty enough to pick up my *Clarion* and my beer, and move to another table.

Under the black top head, the *Clarion* had a series of drop-heads discussing the location of the gambling club ("Apartment on Sherbrooke West Raided as Result of Crime") and the identity of the victim ("C. Winston Wales, Investment Banker, Shot by Unknown Gangster"). There was also one picture on the front page—a picture of Wales, the pathetic little man who had died in the hallway before apartment sixteen.

The story, for which MacArnold had been given a by-line, didn't give much play to the killing. It told how Wales' body was still warm when Framboise and his squad, summoned by an anonymous telephone call, arrived on the scene. It gave a brief review of Wales' life.

Then MacArnold took the bit in his teeth and galloped into the part of the story he had background material to write. He told in minute detail about the gambling club—the high stakes, the wealthy patrons, the luxurious trappings, the free liquor and food. He suggested that Wales might have dropped a roll and started out to call on the cops, only to be stopped by a bullet. He more than hinted that the late unlamented Chesterley had been associated with the joint. And by the time I had followed the story over to the second page, he was holding up his hands and editorializing in holy horror about the state of morals in Montreal, when a club like this could exist undetected and be patronized by the elite, the wealthy, the pillars of the city's business and financial life. He pulled out the *vox humana* stop and labored this point for a good six paragraphs.

On the second page there was also a number of pictures of the club. MacArnold had been on the job, and a *Clarion* reporter had been there while the police were rounding up the found-ins and booking them. They were a very sorry-looking bunch.

I looked. Then, at one picture, I looked more closely. I let out a peal of laughter that woke three sleeping drunks and made the waiter jump as if he'd been goosed.

There, in the picture, standing in front of a sergeant with a notebook, his hands raised angrily to gesture, was my friend James Montgomery.

When I'd finished my quart I left the tavern and went across the street and into the Bank of London. I stamped through the high, hushed, hollow marble halls and accosted the grand ex-cavalry officer who started the twenty elevators. "Mr. MacFaden's office?"

He looked me up and down for hidden weapons, but I'd taken off my shoulder holster. He completed his security check and told me confidentially, "Twenty-third floor. Take the express here on the left, sir."

On the twenty-third floor, straight ahead as I got off the elevator, was a door broad enough for loading hay. It was labelled, "President's Office." I pressed on.

It was only a blind. Inside was a manorial hall, a good two storeys high, wall-to-walled with a dark and doleful rug and panelled in dull mahogany. Around the walls were about sixteen more doors. In the exact centre of this sanctum was a receptionist's desk staffed by a young, sedate, bespectacled girl.

I approached her. I said, "I want to see Mr. MacFaden."

"May I have your name?"

"Russell Teed."

She fumbled at an intercom set. "Was your appointment for this hour, Mr. Teed?" she asked me.

"I don't have an appointment."

All action ceased. "Oh," she said blankly.

"But it is a most urgent matter."

"Personal?"

"Yes."

"You're a personal friend of Mr. MacFaden's?"

"No," I said patiently.

She could be patient too. "Mr. MacFaden is our president, you know," she told me slowly enough so I could spell the words out mentally if I had to do that to understand them. "I'm afraid it's impossible to see him without an appointment. There are many demands on his—"

"Yeah, I know. What do I do to get an appointment? Go back downstairs and open an account in the bank?"

She colored. "Mr. MacFaden's personal secretary is also very busy. Perhaps you could speak to his assistant personal secretary."

"Perhaps I could, and then perhaps I don't want to," I said in a huff. I added quickly, "But I will."

She put her face down and talked surreptitiously into the intercom, and then pointed out a door. I went to it and through it. I was in a small, tidy office facing a girl twice as efficient as the first, but also a good deal prettier.

"Are you MacFaden's assistant personal secretary?" I asked her.

"No, I'm his assistant personal secretary's secretary. What can I do for you?"

"Not a Goddamn thing!" I yelled, "Only let me use your telephone."

She slipped backward out of her chair and retreated

from her desk with an open mouth and a red face. Beside her telephone was a Bank phone directory. I looked up MacFaden, and he was listed.

I dialled his local. I suppose anybody in the city could have done it. In the receiver a dry but pleasant voice said, "MacFaden speaking."

After all that monkey business.

"My name is Russell Teed," I told him. "I have an urgent personal matter to discuss with you right away, if you aren't too busy."

"Never too busy," MacFaden said brusquely. "I'm on the twenty-third floor of the Bank building. How soon can you be here?"

"As soon as I get through the maze that protects your office," I said bitterly. "I'm on the twenty-third floor, too."

When I came back out into the baronial foyer MacFaden was standing in an open doorway. The receptionist gawked at me. I went toward him and followed him into an office no bigger than the average aircraft hangar. There was a board table at one side, but you could set up bowling alleys in the empty space between that and his desk. The desk itself was big enough for a hockey team to practise on.

We sat down. He offered me cigarettes out of a silver box, but I was afraid they might be Turkish so I shook my head politely and pulled out a State Express.

He said, "What is the nature of your business, Mr. Teed?"

"Unpleasant," I said. "I'm a private investigator."

"I hardly expect you are investigating me," he said easily.

"Why? Is all your life an open book?"

He gave me a starchy stare. "Perhaps you'd better tell me why you are here."

"This." I pulled Crawfie's portrait of him from my pocket and skidded it across the desk to him. It only went halfway, so he had to get out of his chair to reach it.

He studied the snap. Then he said, "This is certainly my picture. But I don't know where it was taken, and I don't quite see its significance."

"It was taken at the doorway of an apartment, in a building on Sherbrooke Street West. Its significance is on the front page of this morning's *Clarion*."

"Oh," he said slowly. "I see."

"You were right the first time, Mr. MacFaden. I'm not investigating you. I'm not trying to put you on a spot or embarrass you. But I would like to know two things: first, has it been your habit to gamble at the place this picture was taken?"

He looked at me shrewdly. "I'm sorry to trouble you, but have you some identification? You see my position. If, for instance, you were a reporter masquerading as—"

"Of course." I got out my wallet and showed him the little official ticket the licensing board gives me. It had my name, birthdate, weight, scars, signature, picture and thumbprint—everything but a smear of my blood. It said I was a private investigator, and you could hardly doubt it.

"Thanks." He tossed it back. "Just one more thing. Can I be assured that you aren't working for interests detrimental to me or to my position?"

"Things can get Goddamn complicated, can't they?" I said pleasantly. "Now, to answer that last question of yours, I'd have to ask my second question. And I wanted to clear up the first one first."

"I've already admitted this is a picture of me. Let's assume I admit it was taken where you claim it was—at this gambling place on Sherbrooke."

"Okay. Thank you. My position is this. I know who took the picture—and others like it. I don't know why he took it. The only logical assumption is he wanted to blackmail people who gambled, and whose public position was such they'd pay to keep it quiet."

"Why are you interested in the person who took the picture?"

"Because he's a stinkin' little rat and I want to get something on him."

"You couldn't prove he was a blackmailer. If people were being blackmailed, and were paying off, they'd hardly be willing to take the publicity of a court case."

He seemed to have a logical mind. That's commendable, but sometimes it's troublesome. "I'll amplify," I said patiently. "This person had disappeared. Both his disappearance and his present whereabouts may be explained by these pictures—the one of you, and some others. If I can find out what he's doing with the pictures, maybe I can find him. After that I'll get something on him if I have to beat it out of him. I'm working on a theory that says he's hiding out where he can take the pictures and blackmail his victims."

"I see. Well. What's your second question?"

"Have you been blackmailed?"

"No."

I looked into the polished surface of the desk. His reflection and mine were very clear. His face looked neutral, perhaps a bit expectant as if he expected me to say something more. It certainly didn't look guilty. It didn't look as if he'd just lied to me.

My reflection looked disappointed, or any stronger word you can think of along that line.

"Well, thanks," I said. "I'm sorry I wasted your time."

"I wish I could have helped you. Frankly, I've gambled in that place several times. It's an old vice of mine. But I had no idea that picture was taken. I never saw it before you showed it to me, and certainly it hasn't been used to extort money from me."

"Okay. Thanks."

"If anything further happens, I'll be glad to get in touch with you."

"I'm in the directory," I said. "Russell Teed." I would have given him my number, but he didn't have so much as a memo pad on that clean desk.

"Good morning," I said. "Thank you again."

As I went out he settled back again behind the empty desk and lazily pulled the silver cigarette box toward him. Maybe his personal secretary and his assistant personal secretary were busy, but he wasn't. He just sat there all day, waiting for things like me to happen. It was nice to have enough experience and ability so you could be well paid for working like that.

I went out into the sunlight of Notre Dame Street and kicked the little Morris in the slats until it started. I went home.

Lila was sitting on the chesterfield in my front room, relaxing with all the good things of life I could provide. A flat fifty of my State Express was open beside her, and she was using my best crystal to drink sherry. The sherry bottle was beside her glass; it was the Harvey's Bristol Cream I'd been saving for the next time Royalty called on me.

I said pointedly, "I thought you were going to get dressed and go, right after I left."

"I like it here. I decided to stay."

"Don't get the idea you're a permanent fixture."

"That's a sweet way to talk, after what we've—"

"No lip," I said shortly. "Or I'll give you your five bucks and throw you out on the street."

She got up deliberately and came to me. She hit me across the mouth with the back of her hand. It was meant to hurt, and it did.

"All right, be a complete bastard," she said. "I was just leaving anyway."

"Oh, never mind. Sit down. You can be useful. Anyhow you haven't finished your sherry."

I shoved her back into the chesterfield. I took out the two pictures, the one of Hamish MacFaden and the one of C. Winston Wales, and tossed them to her.

"What do I do with these?"

"What do they mean to you?"

"Nothing at all."

"I guess I should have the *Clarion* delivered here in the mornings."

"I don't get it."

"One of these two was murdered last night. It's all over the front page. It doesn't matter if you don't get anything from them."

"Why should I?"

"They come from the Crawford Foster Studio."

"No kiddin'? He wasn't handling anything like this while I was around. He didn't take pics himself, of course, he just developed the ones we took. And all we took was night club shots."

"He took these," I said. "But I doubt if he showed them to any of you kids. Notice anything about them?"

"Well—They're both taken at the same doorway. What do you want me to notice?"

"Go on. You're doing fine."

"They're both taken from exactly the same spot. But exactly. It's not just that the photographer was standing in the same place both times, but more like the camera was in some kind of rigid mounting. It was in the mounting for both shots."

"That's the kind of thing I want. Anything else?"

"What kind of light was used to take them?" she wondered.

"Don't know. For a guess, they were shot by infra-red flash."

"That's funny. You'd think the light source would be near the camera lens, then."

"You'd think so," I agreed.

"Look at this." She tossed me MacFaden's picture. "Here, the face is lighted from top left." Then she held out the photo of Wales. "In this one, the face is lighted from top right."

"Huh," I grunted. "What do you make of that?"

"What do *you* make of it?"

"Nothing. You're the photographer."

"I'd say the light source, the flash or whatever, was high left on one and high right on the other. Obviously. But that doesn't tie in with an arranged set-up, like you'd have with a rigid camera mount. It's screwy. And there's something else funny about them."

"What?"

She took the pics back from me and studied them again. She shook her head. "I don't know. Something. Maybe it'll come to me later."

"Fine. I'll see you later."

"You kicking me out because I was drinking your good sherry?"

"No. Because I'm going out myself, and I don't want to leave you here to start on the rest of my liquor."

"Awww, Russell," she mooned.

"Careful. I gag easily."

"You were so nice to me earlier this morning."

"It was your idea, not mine. And how I regret it."

"Like me to come back this evening?"

"Sure," I said, "but I haven't got an extra key to the place. Wait just outside the door. I'll be in sometime. Likely."

She slapped me again. Then she kissed me. For just one minute I closed my eyes and made believe it was Elena, but that didn't go on long. After all I'm a big boy, and daddy told me the truth about Santa Claus when I began getting overexpensive ideas.

I put one hand between her major geographic features and pushed her away. "Goodbye," I said. "If you run into Irish Joe again, tell him I'll kill him if he scratches up my car."

"What?"

"Irish Joe."

"Who's he?"

I took her by the hand. "We can spend longer getting nowhere than any two people I know," I said. I led her to the door and put her out, like you put out a cat with bad night habits.

"Sometimes we get somewhere," she said meaningly. She leaned against the door jamb and tried to seduce me with her eyes.

I closed the door. I snapped the latch and did the chain and turned the key in the night lock. Then I took a cold shower.

Chapter Fourteen

I STOOD IN FRONT of Montgomery's apartment door with a bottle of VO rye in one hand, a bottle of Scotch under the same arm, and punched his buzzer for the third time, and he came and opened the door.

"Oh, you," he grunted. "We were in the kitchen finishing lunch. Didn't hear you."

I came in. He didn't invite me in, but he didn't block my way. "What's the idea?" I asked. "I phoned the office and they said you were sick today. I tried to call you here and your line's been busy for an hour."

"It's a two-party line, and my party had teen-age daughters. Daughters, plural. As for the office, it was a lot simpler to say I was sick than to tell them I sat in jail all night." He noticed my load. "I see you brought peace-offerings. Good."

I put the rye down on his hall table, and the Scotch beside it. "These aren't to drink. I brought them with me for safe-keeping. I have a premonition my apartment's going to be burgled."

He looked at the bottles without much interest. "We're drinking beer, anyway. Come on out. I'll sell you all you can drink for fifty cents a bottle."

"Thanks!" I said heartily, the way you thank a guy for treading on your feet in a tram.

He headed for the kitchen and I followed. Sitting at the table with a glass of milk, a bottle of beer and a cup of black coffee before him, was MacArnold. He was drinking deliberately in 1, 2, 3, 1, 2, 3 sequence.

MacArnold's hair was tousled and his face was green from lack of sleep. "Yah. You," he grumped.

"I get a fine reception here. Let me tell you guys I feel just the same way about both of you."

That didn't stir up any fire. I went to the frig and drew myself a quart of Molson. I gave Montgomery fifty cents before opening it. He fooled me. He took the money.

"You want to watch your health," I warned MacArnold. "Are you sure that milk's pasteurized?"

He trained his eyes on me. They were red as a pair of Buick tail-lights. "The new Milton Berle," he said disgustedly. "Tell me, Buster, where were you while all the hell was breaking loose?"

"The last I recall, we were running in opposite directions," I said. "Also, Framboise was travelling away from both of us. Who caught up with you, the boogey man?"

Montgomery broke into the conversation rudely. "Don't think of me," he grated. "Don't let my little troubles worry you. I only went into that gambling hole to help you guys out. What I was supposed to investigate, I don't even know yet. So I start with a century's worth of chips, build it up to sixteen hundred little green lettuce leaves, and what happens? Bingo, you snoops get the place raided. Here. Have some money!" He took a handful of Irish Joe's best twenty-buck ivories from his pocket and tossed them in the air.

"Well, that takes care of your story. Nothing more interesting than to grouse at your own troubles," I said. "Come on, MacArnold, give. What went wrong with your evening?"

"A fine pal you are. I don't see how you missed seeing it," he grumbled. "I get ten yards away from the building and two of Framboise's finest caught up with me and climbed all over me. They brought me back in and accused me of either murdering the guy or helping you do it."

"Aw, too bad," I said.

"Wait until Framboise gets you. I told him you did it."

"He hasn't been looking for me, because I was home all night and nobody broke in on me. That shows how much he believes you."

"Why didn't you help me when I was nabbed, you yellow rat?"

"I was half-a-mile away from there in a fast car before they even caught up with you. I got friends. Tell me just what happened."

MacArnold related, "As soon as Framboise got to the eighth floor and saw the body, he figured we'd pulled a fast one on him, so he sent the two boys right back down in the elevator to get us. They got me, and brought me back up. Framboise had just pushed his nose into fifteen and sixteen. Hanwood wasn't in fifteen—he must have beat it out the back way just as we left. Framboise saw sixteen was a gambling set-up and sent for the vice squad to take the whole bunch in. I was lucky. He left me unwatched for a minute and I got a chance to tip off my editor to what was happening, and get a photographer rushed up."

"What story did you tell Framboise?" I asked.

"Well, not exactly the truth. I admitted we might have kind of been doing a little gambling. We heard the shot and rushed into the hall, there was the body, so we thought it would be healthy to leave."

"Did he get anything on the killing?"

"Nah. After the vice squad booked all the crowd in sixteen as found-ins, Framboise and his men grilled them one by one. Most of them hadn't even heard the shot. Then they trucked them all off to night court."

"Including me," Montgomery said bitterly.

"Incidentally, they didn't get Irish Joe nor his little Indian-faced bum-boy. They booked the monkey who tended the door as the operator of the joint."

"Heh," I said. "It was some kind of a put-up job. You heard the sirens approaching before the echoes of the killing shot had even died away. Somebody wanted to be sure that body was found right away. The cops were told about the killing before it happened, for sure. They got an anonymous phone call, didn't they?"

"Yes, Framboise said so."

"Man or woman?"

"Man."

"Saying what?"

"A man had been shot and killed on the eighth floor at that address. Those were the exact words of the message—shot and killed. I checked."

"So the guy makes the phone call with the gun in his hand, hangs up and pops off Mr. Wales. How did he know Wales would be leaving just at that moment?"

"Inside job," Montgomery suggested. "The fact that Irish Joe got away supports that theory. Somebody—inside apartment sixteen—waits until Wales is just leaving, calls the cops, shoots Wales, and then tips off Irish Joe. Or maybe four different guys did those four jobs, but if so they all knew and liked each other."

"Sounds logical," I said. "Also sounds completely screwy."

"Why?" he wanted to know.

MacArnold said, "I see what you mean. The last thing Irish Joe would want would be the cops at his front door. He'd want time to pick up the body and throw it out the nearest window. Also he'd sooner have it found the next morning than right then."

"Maybe," I said slowly. "And maybe not."

"You got an idea?"

"Yeah, a small glimmer. But it doesn't hold water yet. It isn't even tight enough to hold marbles. Don't ask me."

"To hell with all this," Montgomery snarled, opening another quart for himself. "What about my sixteen hundred iron men?"

"*Your* sixteen hundred?" MacArnold said in mock surprise. "What about my century? That was what you started with."

"And there's the matter of my fifty-dollar fine."

"I guess you better tap the *Clarion* expense money for another fifty," I told MacArnold.

"You tapped it for the last hundred. Remember?"

"Oh—oh. I'd forgotten that," Montgomery said unpleasantly. "Tell you what. I'll give you back your hundred in chips and you give me the money."

"Like hell," I said.

They converged on me. I didn't put down my beer fast enough and most of it went over me as they deposited me flat on the kitchen floor. MacArnold sat on my head and Montgomery sat on my feet and took out my wallet. He counted out five twenties and gave two to MacArnold. "The extra ten to me is for the indignity of my arrest," he said, and stowed the money away. He put five chips politely in my pocket.

They got off me. "All right, old man, you can get up now," Montgomery said.

He was damn casual for a man who was getting a black eye, but perhaps he didn't realize he'd been hit.

I found a towel and mopped off the beer that hadn't soaked in. I refilled my glass from a new bottle, and gave Montgomery another fifty cents. "Oh, that's all right, old man," he said, but he took the fifty cents again.

I sat down. "Look, we're getting nowhere at a hell of a clip," I complained. "Listen while I review this thing.

"Chesterley is killed. Probably by Irish Joe and the

Indian. Probably because the latter two plus Crawfie Foster are planning to blackmail the apartment sixteen customers and Chesterley objects it's bad for business.

"I am attacked to suggest to me I shouldn't take too active an interest in the case. Priscilla is attacked because she tumbled somehow to Crawfie's end of the deal.

"Then Wales is shot. God alone knows why."

"Sounds like a good summary," MacArnold said. "I agree."

"Sure. There aren't more than ten things wrong with it. First, we can't hang the mountain killing on Irish Joe—no witnesses. Second, we don't know where Crawfie is so we can't get anything out of him. Third, we don't know how the pictures are being taken—he doesn't live in apartment fifteen, and he can't just sit in the corridor and snap them.

"Fourth, who attacked Priscilla? Fifth, we don't know the pictures are being used for blackmail. That's a big hole in the theory. I just talked to Hamish MacFaden and nobody's been blackmailing him. Sixth, why was Wales killed? I could go on."

"All right, go on," Montgomery said. "I haven't heard all this before. It's interesting."

"That's about all it is. Okay. Seventh, how did Priscilla find Crawfie and latch onto the picture I found at her place? Eighth, we haven't established any connection yet between Crawfie and Irish Joe—except theoretically. Ninth, there was supposed to be a third partner in the gambling business, beside Chesterley and Irish Joe, and we don't know who that was unless it was the Indian."

"Ten? You said ten."

"Tenth, why the hell did Irish Joe steal my Riley?" I shouted. "You satisfied? That's the list."

Montgomery got up solemnly and left the room. He was back in a minute with a large blank pad and a fountain pen. "Obviously, what we need is a plan of action," he said.

"Good man," MacArnold applauded.

"We put down what has to be done, how we can approach each of these problems, and then we all start to work. We'll report back to Teed's apartment—it's more central—tomorrow morning. That gives us time to accomplish something."

"Fine," I said. "MacArnold can get away with that because his editor wants him to work on this case. But will Associated Chemical be happy that you spend your time trying to solve crime?"

"I'll be sick for a few days," Montgomery said callously. "I've been sick before for less reason."

He scribbled on the pad for a few minutes. "All right, I've got the ten problems down. Now let's start to work. Who wants to do what? Teed, your privilege to choose first."

"I'll try to find Crawfie," I said. "He's my main interest in this case, at the moment. That'll take me till tomorrow morning, if I can do it at all."

"Okay. MacArnold?"

"I think I might look into the connection between Foster and Irish Joe. I have a hunch I might get something if I start back at Louie Two's again, do some pumping there, and see where it leads me."

"Okay." Montgomery scanned his list. "I know what I want to do," he decided. "Only, I don't know how to approach the investigation. Maybe I'll go to Louie Two's with MacArnold for a beginning."

"What you investigating?"

"The third partner. That fascinates me."

"Why?"

"Because I can't think who it might be, except one of us."

MacArnold and I spoke simultaneously. I said, "How the devil do you figure that?" and he said, "What the hell do you mean?"

"It's just an idea," Montgomery said mildly. "A lot of things that happened followed from information only we three had. I don't have to count over the cases. You all know what I mean."

We looked at him with our mouths open.

He said, "To protect all of us, I want to find the third partner. I don't think he's one of us. But I don't think he's the Indian either."

Chapter Fifteen

It was only four in the afternoon, and Louie Two's never opened before dinner so MacArnold and Montgomery stayed to kill a few more beers. I carried my bottles of rye and Scotch carefully back out to the Morris and started downtown.

I found a place to park the Morris on Stanley Street and walked along Burnside to Peel, then down to the Elephant Tavern. I sat down at a table near the door, ordered my quart, and engaged the waiter in conversation when he brought it.

"Haven't see you here before," I began.

"My name's Artie," he volunteered. "I been here three years. I'm on the day shift."

"All the time?"

"Yeah. Finish at six every day."

"How good's your memory, Artie?" I slipped him a buck.

He took the bill. "Awful good."

"End of last month, a guy moved out of one of the offices overhead here. He skipped owing me some money. I'm trying to find out where he went."

"You want to describe him? Maybe he come in here for a drink sometimes in the days."

"Not the type. I'm interested in the trucker that moved him out. If I can latch onto him, I can find out where he sent his stuff, at least."

"When did you say he moved out?"

"End of last month."

"I think—Yeah! There was this truck parked out here for a couple hours on the thirty-first. I remember I noticed it when I skipped out at lunchtime to cash my pay cheque. Two guys were loading a big shiny machine on the truck.

Looked like an oversize pop-corn machine."

"That would be his drum-drier, for prints. That's the right guy. Okay. It's worth another five bucks if you can remember the name on the truck."

Artie wrinkled his brow. He half-opened his mouth and rubbed his rough jaw with his rough hand. After a while a light seemed to dawn, and his face cleared up. He got nervous, though, and stood first on one foot and then on the other. He didn't say anything.

I pulled out the five and waved it at him. Maybe that was what he was waiting for.

"Aw, hell," he said and shook his head sadly. "I could gyp you, but I wouldn't do that. I can't take your five bucks. There wasn't any name on the truck at all."

"There must have been! The law requires it."

"It was an old, beat-up truck. Maybe there was a name scratched on the door toward the street, but there wasn't no name on this side. I thought back, and I remember. Sure."

I put the five away, but I gave him another buck for being honest. That satisfied him. I got good service for the next few hours. I sat bathed in gloom and floated myself in beer. I had a sandwich there in the Elephant, in lieu of dinner. I tried to think what else I could do. It got dark. I couldn't think of anything else to do.

I had a small thought. It wasn't a very good thought, but it was the only one I had.

Crawfie had left, in Priscilla's room, the photograph of Hamish MacFaden I'd found there. Crawfie hadn't even looked for it. That might have meant he didn't know Priscilla had it. On the other hand, maybe it meant he was planning to come back for it another time.

I pushed myself and my skinful of beer away from the table and meandered back to the Morris. As I said, it was a small thought, not very good. All I could do to test it was sit in front of Priscilla's place through the night. It seemed like an awful waste of time, but I had nothing else to do with my time just then.

At least there were two bottles of whiskey in the car.

A few minutes later I drew up in front of Priscilla's. I sat for five or ten minutes before the chill began to get me. It was a cool night, the Morris top was down, and I was wearing only a jacket—no top coat. I began to get cold. The more I thought about the warming bottles in the glove compartment, the colder I got. I could have put up the car-top, but unscrewing a bottle cap was a lot less work.

I let considerable Scotch gurgle down the gullet. I felt better immediately. I put the bottle back and resumed my watch.

Nothing at all was happening. The street was black and still, with very few cars passing and none at all stopping. I was parked just above the old house Priscilla had lived in, behind another car. I'd chosen the spot to provide a bit of camouflage.

The car in front of me was a black convertible with its top down. I studied it idly. It wasn't an American car, it was English. Probably a . . .

I looked closer. It was a Riley.

I vaulted out of the Morris without stopping to open the door. I went over and prowled around the Riley.

It wasn't just A Riley. It was Riley. It was my car!

My overpowering rage was eased by the fact Riley seemed to have taken it all very well. I couldn't really tell until I heard his motor, but at least his fenders weren't scratched and his leather upholstery wasn't scuffed.

I checked. His keys weren't in the dash, but I had a spare set in my wallet. I got them out and opened the door. Then

I hauled myself back with a jerk.

Much as I wanted Riley back right away, I'd have to use him for a decoy. Whoever was driving Riley was likely inside Priscilla's room, combing it for the picture. I could wait and pounce on them as they came back out to drive Riley away. Or I could let them drive off, and follow where they led me. That sounded best, if hardest to do. The thought of an alien hand on Riley's wheel made me wince.

I went back to the Morris. This time I didn't sit behind the wheel; I sat on the floor behind the front seat. It was a tight squeeze but I did it, sitting sideways. I was hidden.

I didn't have long to wait. About fifteen minutes later, a slinking figure edged out the door of Priscilla's house. It wasn't a figure built for successful slinking. It was a pear-shaped body, narrow-shouldered with a bulging paunch and fat hips, shaping off abruptly to weak, skinny legs and mincing little feet. He was dressed in sloppy, crumpled clothes. The beam of a street-light caught his face and glinted on big, flat spectacles that framed his eyes.

The little rat had put on weight in the stir, and he was some sloppier than he used to be. But I was sure of him even before he came closer and got into the Riley.

It was Crawfie Foster. At last.

He turned on the lights, and started Riley. I breathed a prayer of thanks. Riley's engine sounded just fine.

Then he sped away from the curb and I hopped into the driver's seat of the Morris and started after him. I followed him as he circled down to St. Catherine, around and up to Sherbrooke, and then west.

It was tricky, keeping up with Riley and Foster. On a crowded street I would have had a good chance. But the road was clear and even a poor driver like Crawfie could hardly help drawing well ahead. He could burst into speed between traffic lights while the Morris was laboring to get up momentum. Going through Westmount, where the lights are thick and too quickly timed, I got three or four blocks behind him. I made up some time zooming through the left side of safety zones and had him in sight as he turned right, up Decarie. After that I lost him. The Morris was as much trouble to pull up the hill as a bicycle, and about as fast.

I remembered some curses I'd forgotten since I was discharged from the army. If I'd missed my chance to get Riley back, on the hope of following Foster, and was going to lose him now, I was about as bright as the moon in the daytime. Because I was not only losing Riley—that was bad enough. I'd had Crawfie where I could almost reach out and grab him, and I was losing him too.

After I got to the top of the hill the Morris began to accelerate and I bore on down Decarie, through Snowdon Junction. I went right through three traffic lights—one green, the next one yellow, and the third one red. A taxi-driver yelled at me but no sirens started.

North and north I went, past the Garland tram terminal, down into the rail underpass and up, through the neon-brilliant sunset strip of drive-ins and night clubs. The Morris approached the Cote de Liesse traffic circle, and I still hadn't spotted Riley ahead of me.

But something flashed by at the side of the road. I braked and looked back over my shoulder. Riley was parked at the curb, in front of a dark and deserted refreshment stand.

I shut off the lights, closed in to the curb, and backed until I was a few yards from Riley. I cut the engine, got a flashlight from the shelf under the dash, and crept back to my own car. It was empty.

This was a deserted area. A few shut and silent industrial plants were grouped on the other side of the broad road.

Cars went by at intervals, at high speed. This side of the road was mostly open fields stretching all the way to the Town of Mount Royal, except for the small roadside canteen.

I was alone, I was without my gun, and I was worried. Crawfie was likely inside the canteen, or behind it. That didn't worry me. But probably he had come here to meet someone, and I didn't relish the idea of uneven odds.

However, Crawfie couldn't have had any idea I was following him. I had surprise, and if necessary concealment on my side.

I took a firm grip on the flashlight and went on tip-toe over quiet grass toward the canteen. I put my ear against a boarded-up window. No sound inside.

I edged around to the back of the shack. As I rounded the final corner I stopped and listened again. There was absolute silence.

Where the hell had Crawfie gone? Not far, because the Riley was parked right in front.

I turned on the flashlight and swept the beam in front of me.

About ten feet away, at eye-level, it picked up the white-bandaged face of Irish Joe's Indian, the shining big round lenses of Crawfie Foster's spectacles and his foolish gaping mouth, and the blue jaw of Irish Joe. Before I cut the light Irish Joe's hand was diving in his jacket for his gun.

I cut and run.

Five feet from the Morris, I took off the sod and landed behind the wheel. They were pounding behind me. The Morris started like a charm and I zoomed away before they could even get a hand on it. I gunned it in low, shifted up and gunned again, and was shifting into high when I hit the deepest pothole in the Province of Quebec. It jarred my teeth. I was afraid a spring had gone, but the Morris travelled on.

There was only one thing wrong. The Morris was travelling on momentum alone. Its motor wasn't running, and slowly it rolled to a stop.

Maybe the bump had knocked the ignition out. I flipped the key off and on again, and jerked the starter. The starter turned the motor, but it didn't catch.

They were pounding along the road behind me.

I jerked the starter again with no more result. Time was running out. I jumped from the Morris and ran for it. I made a pretty good race, too, but they were too close to me.

About five yards from the Morris, something hit me like a bag of cement swung on the end of a rope. I was knocked right off my feet and fell, half on the road and half on the grass. Then something the size of a Percheron stallion fell on my neck.

That would be Irish Joe, no doubt.

There were more pounding steps, and something hit my legs. The blow came just where my shin-bones lay across the curb. I felt as if somebody had laid me on the tracks and the six-fifteen express had passed by.

I struggled to throw Irish Joe off my shoulders. The minute I moved, an exquisite pain flashed through my left leg and I collapsed like a tar-paper shack in an earthquake.

Three cars passed down the road in rapid succession. They were going fast and their lights hardly touched the scene of battle.

The Riley's horn blatted out. Crawfie called, "come back, and let's get out of here. It's too public."

Another car came by, going more slowly. Its lights lit us up for a good ten seconds. With one eye I saw Irish Joe lifting a gun over my head.

"This time," he snarled, "don't wake up!"

I saw bright stars, and the everlasting night.

Chapter Sixteen

I SUPPOSE THERE WERE very few good things you could ever say about Irish Joe, but you could say this. Whether by accident or design, he missed the sore spot in my skull and hit somewhere else. And while it was no love-tap, it didn't break anything.

I woke up. I didn't know what time it was. Frankly, I didn't much care; I had other things to think about.

I was lucky in one way. I didn't have much of a headache. Maybe I was getting immune to sluggings. Or maybe Irish Joe was out of breath from catching me and hadn't hit as hard as he meant. Anyhow, I felt pretty good. I still had enough alcohol in my blood-stream to ward off chill and keep me from thinking morose thoughts. I stretched my arms and yawned to open my eyes, and I sat up.

I fainted.

When I woke up again I was lying on my back. This time I behaved more cautiously. I put weight on my arms and eased myself to a sitting position.

I found if I moved my left leg, or did anything that resulted in it moving, the pain was intense enough to nauseate me. A spasm of pure pain would start from my leg, settle in the pit of my stomach, would gather itself together like a crouching cougar and try to broad-jump.

I got slowly erect on my good foot. I had some bad moments as the left leg was leaving the ground, but finally I was upright and it hung down beside my right. I hopped toward the Morris.

I took one hop, that is. The jar raised so much protest from the damaged leg I blacked out for a moment on my feet. I don't know how I stayed on them.

So no more hopping. So I inched the rest of the way to the Morris, more or less like a man trying to progress over rough, sanded ice on one skate. When I got to the car I found there was no hope of getting inside. I could reach the glove compartment, though. I grabbed a bottle. I have seldom done more damage to a Scotch bottle in one swig.

I wondered what was wrong with the Morris. The starting motor had worked, after the engine cut out, so the battery wasn't dead. It couldn't be out of gas because I'd filled it in the afternoon. Maybe a gas line had snapped when I hit the hole. To hell with it, it was an academic problem anyhow. If the thing was running, I couldn't get in to drive it.

Slowly and with infinite care, supporting myself on the car, I worked around to the outer side of the auto. I braced myself and got an arm free to flag down a passerby.

In the space of half an hour only six cars went by. I guess it was early morning. They were all going fast, and for me they didn't even slow up. Maybe they thought I was waving to wish them a happy journey.

The seventh car was a low-slung racy convertible, with the top down. It began to slow as soon as I started waving, and halted just abreast of the Morris. I saw then it was a Jaguar.

An unpleasantly familiar voice said, "Well, well. Hello, Teed."

"Okay, on your way, Hanwood," I told him. "I'll flag down the next guy who passes."

Elena was with him. She leaned out her side of the car. "Is anything wrong?"

"Not a thing. Go on, get going. You spoil my view."

She saw the way I was holding my leg. And my clothes hadn't improved any by rolling in the sod. She opened her door. “I’m going to see what’s wrong.”

“Elena, get back in here,” Paul Hanwood cracked.

“Just wait a minute, Paul.”

“No, I won’t wait. Get back in or I’ll leave you here. And if he’s having motor trouble, you’ll have a long walk home.”

She looked me up and down. I was having a little trouble hanging on to the car. She turned to face Paul. “All right, go along if you want to,” she said coldly.

“I’m warning you. Elena—”

“Aw, get out,” I snorted. “Or else come here where I can reach you, Paul.”

Hanwood began to get the idea he wasn’t wanted. He reached over, slammed the door Elena had left open, and left with a snarl of exhaust fumes.

“What’s wrong?”

“Well, to begin with, the car won’t work,” I said bitterly. “That I don’t mind too much, except it stopped working just in time to get me a broken leg.”

“Oh! What happened?”

“I was jumped. Or more precisely, I was jumped on. My leg happened to be lying across the curb.”

She paled. I thought she was going to faint. “Easy!” I snapped. “It didn’t hurt. I just want to get out of here.”

“What’s wrong with the car?” she asked, coming back strong.

I explained. She frowned. Then she went around the car, unhitched the hood latch, and lifted the hood.

“What do you know about those things?”

“Enough. I was friendly with a man who had one, in Rome.”

“Well, it’s nothing obvious that’s wrong. I’m not out of gas and the battery is okay.”

“Flashlight?”

"You might find it over there on the grass. Just ahead there, where the sod is chewed up."

She retrieved it and came back to duck her head over the engine. "Hah!" she said triumphantly. "Pliers?"

"Here in the luggage compartment."

She hauled out the pliers and was busy for a minute. I hooked one arm over the side of the Morris, reached with the other, and just managed to get the Scotch bottle again. I lowered its level another inch and put it on the back seat.

Elena switched out the flashlight and slammed down the hood. "It should run," she said. "It is a fault of some of these cars. Their wiring system is not robust enough for the rough Canadian roads."

She got in the Morris and tried the motor. After whining for a minute, it started. "The lead to the fuel pump had loosened," she told me.

"What do you mean? The fuel pump runs off the manifold."

"Not in these cars. It is electric."

I shrugged. I had thought up several items in favor of Elena, but I hadn't expected her to be mechanically useful. I felt a little deflated. Any man would. Even without a broken leg, I'd be going to get a tow-truck, not finding out what was wrong.

Then I stopped blaming myself and blamed the car. It had let me down when I needed it most. It would be a long time before I'd trust that particular Morris again. I wanted Riley back.

"Well—shall we go? Get in," Elena said.

"Get in, she says," I muttered.

"Can you—?"

"No. I can't."

She opened the door from inside the car and hauled me in by brute strength. I was surprised how strong she was. I concentrated on holding my leg with both hands so it wouldn't be jarred. I got in, or mostly in. We couldn't close the door on my side, but none of me was dragging on the ground.

"Not that I'm a back-seat driver," I said, "but go very, very slow. And if you see any bumps, stop, so I can get out and hop past them. I'd sooner."

"We should put a splint on that leg. I am afraid you will compound the fracture."

"I'm holding it like a vise. Keep going, unless you notice I've fainted."

We drove—very, very slowly—to the nearest set of lights, which proved to be a service station. I gave Elena Danny Moore's number, and she went in to call him.

She was back in a minute. "What did he say?" I asked.

"He told me what time it is. It is four o'clock. When I explained our problem he said he would meet us at the hospital."

"Why not his office?"

"He wants you x-rayed, and he must have facilities to put on a cast."

"Oh, all right. Let's go. Slowly."

"He wondered if we had anaesthetic. I said yes, you were only halfway through the bottle."

She started the car smoothly and we inched out into the traffic lane and easily down the road.

"Aw, hell!" I snapped.

Her foot lifted from the gas. "You have pain?"

"I have more than pain. I've got a rotten feeling of disgust about this whole case. This case is three stinking problems that tied themselves up into one, and I haven't the answer to any part of it. Tonight I almost got my car back, almost caught Crawfie Foster, located Irish Joe—and then muffed the whole thing by being a damn fool. I ought to give up investigating and go to work for a living."

"What is the case? I don't understand."

"It began with a killing on Mount Royal—"

"Oh, yes, Paul told me about that. The day he introduced us. He thought you would investigate it."

"I didn't mean to, but I got involved. The two lugs who probably killed Chesterley on Mount Royal came to see me the next night and worked on me. Then a young girl got shot, and it developed that it was connected with the same case. But last night—that was the puzzler."

"The killing—outside Paul's door?"

"Yeah. It's tied in too. But how? And why was the guy killed? I don't know."

"How is Paul involved in this?"

"I'll bite. How?"

"Do you not think he is involved?"

"I didn't say he was."

"The murder took place just outside his door. Besides—you and your friend were in his apartment. You went in there to look for something."

"We went in there to look for somebody else. We didn't have any idea Paul lived there. One thing's sure: he didn't kill Wales. I was looking right at him when Wales was shot."

"Then—"

"The killing was in front of Paul's door, but it was also in front of the door of an apartment used as a gambling club. That's the tie-in."

"I see."

"Do you care if Paul is mixed up in the business?"

She drew a deep breath and looked very stern. "I don't care what he's mixed up in," she said. "I don't intend to see him again. Not ever."

Chapter Seventeen

I PLANTED THE CRUTCHES firmly and carefully, and lunged forward out of the automatic elevator into my corridor. One crutch tip caught in the edge of the elevator shaft and skidded, and I wound up with my nose nuzzling the rough plaster at the far side of the corridor. My comments on this started right back at the ancestry of the guy who invented the first crutch and went on for several minutes.

"Shhh!" Elena chuckled. "It's six a.m. You'll wake up your neighbors."

It was six, all right. I never knew it took so long to put on a plaster cast, and I never knew what a sloppy job it was either. When Danny Moore got through with me he looked like a drunken paperhanger.

I said, "To hell with the neighbors. How do you learn to walk on these pixilated things, anyway?"

"You are doing very well. But watch the leg. The Doctor said to put no weight on it until—"

"I know, I know. Feel in my left jacket pocket and you'll find my apartment key."

She was carrying the Scotch in one hand, the rye in the other. She set them on the floor and got my keys out. Then she went down the corridor and tried to open Mrs. MacEchran's door with them.

"Hey, you've got an awfully poor memory!" I roared.

"The door is opening."

The door was opening because Mrs. MacEchran was opening it from the inside. She stood there at the door, all red hair and 1890 flannel night gown, and gaped at Elena. Then she saw me, and for the first time in some years, her dreams had come true. I bet she'd prayed for something like this for the past two nights. She looked at me and my broken leg, and a toothless grin spread over her face until you'd think her hooked nose would fall in the crack. Then she began to laugh.

I wanted to throw a crutch at her, but Elena was in the way. "Go back to bed, you old bat!" I yelled. I started toward my own door. The way I walked on crutches made her rev up her laughter like a plane engine guns up before take-off.

Elena wasn't doing anything constructive. I got to her door and pulled it shut in Mrs. MacEchran's battered old face, and retrieved my keys. Then we went into my place.

Five minutes later we were comfortable in my living room, with drinks and cigarettes. I was stretched out on the chesterfield and Elena sat on the floor and leaned against it.

She yawned.

"About time you thought of getting some sleep," I said.

"About time," she agreed.

"If I didn't have a broken leg, you could sleep here."

"I will stay anyway," she said calmly.

"Seems like an awful waste," I sighed. "Why bother?"

"You have adopted me. There is nowhere I can go. I meant what I said, I am through with Paul."

"Were you living with him?"

"No, I had my own apartment. But he was paying its rent."

"Are you moving in with me because you like me, or because you're fed up with Paul?"

With considerable dignity she said, "I refuse to answer that directly. You must guess what you wish. I am moving in for the moment because of circumstances."

"Okay. The why of it doesn't matter much—as long as I'm in this cast."

"Tomorrow—no, I mean today—will be busy. First I

find a job. Then I find a place to live."

"Oh, never mind. Stay here."

"On what terms?" she asked coldly.

"I want you to teach me to speak Italian."

"I want a straight answer, not an evasion."

I rose up on one elbow. I gave her a direct look and there should have been plenty in my eyes because there was plenty in my thoughts, even if it was hard to say it properly.

"You know something? You're the most beautiful girl I ever saw. I fell in love with your looks the first time I saw you in the Trafalgar. I started scheming to get you away from Hanwood right then."

"And now I have come of my own accord, you're not sure you want me after all?"

"All right, so I'm saying this wrong. Look, Elena, get it straight. I want you. I dream about you nights. If you came into this country illegally and have to go back to Italy, I'll go back with you. But let me be sure I'm your choice—not just an alternate."

Her hand reached up to caress my hair and worked its way down to the back of my neck, warm and soft. "I hate Hanwood," she whispered. "I've hated him—since I first saw you."

I left my plaster cast where it was but the rest of me moved into her arms. We kissed the way people kiss who have loved in times gone by, and been reunited after long separation.

"Oh, Russell," she breathed. "I have wanted you too."

There was a loud and raucous noise. A throat had been cleared.

"Hi beg your pardon." The words were sorry, but the voice wasn't. The voice was sarcastic. It was the voice of Framboise.

He said, "Hi regret, Ma'm'selle, that I also want 'im. I

want 'im right at this moment. You can 'ave him later."

We broke it up. "When will I learn to lock my door?" I asked the assembled company. It was corny, but perhaps better than nothing to show Framboise how I felt.

"Could we speak in private?" Framboise wanted to know.

"Sure. Just come here and carry me into another room."

"I will go," Elena said. "It is time. I have much to do."

Framboise bowed politely. He didn't try to stop her. I would have but I couldn't.

The door had hardly shut behind her when he started on me. He was mad. Even Framboise would have commented on my plaster cast, if very pressing things weren't on his mind. He started by throwing a copy of yesterday morning's *Clarion* at me.

"*Regarde!* You have seen this?"

"I've read the front page, if that's what you mean."

"*Oui.* I mean the story of MacHarnold, about the killing of Wales. You *comprends* why I am angry, eh?"

I was tired of his yelling. "Go pour yourself a beer, and let the foam cool you off," I snapped at him. "Stop this big attack on me. I don't know why you're mad, and moreover I don't care. I have my own troubles."

He sat down wearily in the nearest chair. "I can't 'ave a beer," he complained. "Hi'm on duty until eight. You know t'at. I'm t'e night man who gets all t'e dirty jobs, like ones you and MacArnold are mixed into."

"So what have we done now?"

"Concealed hevidence. MacArnold's story says t'ere is a connection between Wales' killing an' the death of Chesterley on top t'e mountain."

"Sure, and if you'd been half on the bit you would have turned it up yourself," I said calmly. "Look, it's almost eight. Go get a beer. You need one. Bring me one too."

He gave in. He went to the kitchen and came back with two quarts. He gave me mine and then sat down wearily and was silent while he went through two glasses. After he finished them he was much calmer. "Do me a very big favor, please," he begged. "Jus' go t'rough the whole story from t'e beginning. Slowly."

"I doubt if I can. I've been up all night. I'm too tired."

"It's too complicated a story for you to tell?"

"Not so much that. But MacArnold and I have done quite a bit of work on this thing. We've found out a few things, but they don't add up, so we haven't told you. When I spin the story you'll start fighting about that."

Framboise contemplated his beer glass. "Hokay," he said finally, in resignation. "Hi promise I don't get tough wit' you for holding out on me. So long as you tell me everyt'ing right now."

I found my State Express and lit myself a fag. As I drew slowly at it I said, "You can have the whole story—what there is of it. Maybe you can make more of it than I can. I'm stymied. But before I begin, what have you been doing all this time? Who've you pulled in on your investigations?"

"On w'at case? Chesterley, or the Wales killing?"

"Both of 'em."

"On Chesterley, I mus' admit, we 'ave nothing. T'is Chesterley was a fool who wen' alone for a walk on the mountain. Someone attacked 'im—"

"Two people attacked him. Someone held his hands while a second beat him with a sap. He couldn't have been mashed up that badly otherwise."

"Hokay, two people attacked 'im. Well—t'at's common enough on the mountain. No matter 'ow much we patrol it. In t'is case, no robbery. Probably t'e crooks are scared off before t'ey can rob 'im."

"I doubt it. It's pretty hard to scare thugs off so fast they don't stop to tear a wallet out of the victim's pocket. Anyway, why the terrific beating? If they were bent on robbing Chesterley, why didn't they just lay him cold and then rifle his pockets?"

"T'ey were afraid he'd recognize t'em later."

"After seeing them once, in the dark, on the mountain? Come off it. Anyway, there's a better explanation. But what about Wales?"

"Wales was an investment banker, wealt'y, well-known. No enemies we can fin'. T'e only guess jus' now is he was cleaned in t'is gambling hole an' t'reatened to inform us. So 'e was eliminated on 'is way out."

"That's the only idea you've got?"

"*Oui*. Now, your story."

"Well, it all seems to revolve around the gambling apartment on Sherbrooke Street. That place was run by three men: a character named Irish Joe, who is about six feet four and couldn't keep his face looking clean if he shaved on the hour. A second character, named Chesterley—"

"*Sacré!* W'ere did you find t'at out?"

"MacArnold found it out. From confidential sources."

Framboise shook his head sadly. "T'e only lead we 'ad on Chesterley was 'is wife, and she swore 'e was a speculator by profession."

"Likely what he told her."

"So you t'ink—"

"That Chesterley was getting profits from the gambling house which Irish Joe and his partner would sooner split between themselves. So Irish Joe and an experienced assistant followed him around until he got foolish."

"Who is t'is assistant? T'e third partner?"

"I don't know whether he's a partner or not, but I know

him. He's a skinny little guy with a face dark as the Pakistani. He has a very good aim with a sap and when I saw him last he was covered with bandages trying to heal up the results of meeting a broken kitchen chair."

"W'ere did you get t'is detail?"

"That was what happened just after Chesterley was killed. Somebody warned 'em I was thinking of taking on the case, so they paid me a little visit. That was why I had a broken head the last time you came here to talk to me."

"W'o is t'e third partner in the gambling 'ouse?" An' how do you know there are t'ree?"

"Confidential information again. Says there are three boys on it, but doesn't give the third. I'll give you my guesses in a minute. Now, from a few years back, do you remember Crawfie Foster?"

He thought a minute. "Oh, *oui*. 'E was mixed up in t'at dope ring w'en we solved the Sark case."

"He's out of stir. I started looking for him just after the Chesterley murder because he'd skipped from his current address owing a client of mine some money. I didn't find him but I found he'd been taking pictures of characters as they left this gambling apartment—the one where Wales was killed. That connected Crawfie Foster with Irish Joe and hence with Chesterley as well. How? I don't exactly know."

Framboise was slowly getting red. He looked like a Christmas cracker about to snap. "*Maudit cochon*—" he began.

"Ah—ah!" I cautioned. "Don't get upset. Remember, you start a fight and I stop talking."

"You blame me for getting mad? W'en I came to hinvestigate t'e shooting of t'e Dover girl, you tol' me you t'ought Crawfie Foster mebbe 'ad done it. Already t'en you knew t'ere was a link between Chesterley an' Foster—t'rough Irish Joe—but you denied t'at to me!"

"I just avoided the question. I didn't know enough then to do you any good. I would just have confused you. Even now I doubt I can do you much good with what I know."

Framboise went out and got another beer to help him keep himself under control. He came back and said, "Well. Continue."

"Up to the night Wales was killed—"

"An' hanother t'ing," Framboise interrupted. "You didn't wait for me to come t'at night. You were right t'ere at t'e death of Wales, an' you skipped out before—"

"Up to the night Wales was killed," I repeated calmly, while he ducked his mug back into the beer, "it stacked up something like this. Seemed likely that Irish Joe and Crawfie Foster had made a deal. Crawfie would snap shots of the departing gamblers, and the pics would be used for blackmail. Likely Chesterley wouldn't agree to the scheme, which would be the reason he was rubbed out. Priscilla Dover tumbled to it somehow because I found one of these snaps in her room—"

"An' didn't tell me," Framboise almost sobbed.

"And so we had the whole series of incidents linked up, and a plausible theory to explain everything."

"No proof. But the t'eory sounds pretty good," he agreed.

"Yeah? You want to know what happened to it? First of all, the spot where Crawfie should have been sitting to take the shots turned out to be a private apartment with a solid oak door you couldn't shoot anything through but x-ray pictures. Figure that one out if you can; I can't. Second, I call on the most important guy whose picture's been snapped and he's never ever been approached to buy them back. If the pics weren't taken to be used as blackmail, why were they taken?"

"Hah," grunted Framboise. He put down his empty

glass and rested his chin on his hand, so he looked like The Thinker in a blue serge suit.

"Add to that the death of Wales," I continued. "Now, one of the snaps Crawfie took was of Wales. Among other things, it means Wales was in the place before his fatal visit there. He was known in the place. If he was a type who might be difficult about calling cops, he'd never have gotten back in. So much for your theory, but who's got any others?"

"Not me," Framboise admitted.

"I got one. Just one. Perhaps Wales was the unknown third partner in the place—if it wasn't Irish Joe's little Indian assistant, and if it wasn't Crawfie himself. That could explain why Wales was shot, but it doesn't explain a lot of other—"

Somebody sneezed. It wasn't exactly close at hand, but it was somewhere in the apartment. Framboise got quietly out of his chair and put his back to a wall, away from the doors to the living room. He pulled his gun slowly from its holster. He wasn't scared or jumpy, but he was being cautious.

"Oh, fine," I whispered to him. "Leave me lying here with a broken leg while you start a gun fight. Who do you expect'll get shot?"

He put his finger to his lips for silence.

I heard a click from the hallway; it was the latch of my hall closet door opening. That made me unhappy because the hall closet was where I kept my gun.

Steps clicked up the hall, and then a girl wandered into the room. She was very attractive, brunette, with a wonderful, slim, big-breasted figure. Her name was Lila.

"Good evening," she said. "Or rather good morning." She looked at Framboise. "Put the gun away, Mister. I'm deadly, but guns aren't effective against that."

"I see w'at you mean," said Framboise. She had on a dress that had been too tight when it was new, and had shrunk a bit in washing. Framboise looked hard at her. Only a cad would hope for a button to pop, but he was no gentleman.

"Pardon me for interrupting," she said politely. "I got tired waiting. Mind if I use the little girl's room?"

I gestured weakly with one hand and she left us.

"T'is is your busy night," Framboise grinned. "I can't t'ink up any more questions to hask you. I go home an' sleep, w'en I wake up I t'ink some more about t'is t'ing. I will be back to see you."

"Sweet dreams."

"You get some sleep too," he advised me. "Wit' two brunettes like t'ose, you need your strengt'."

I threw a crutch at him, but he was gone.

Lila stayed in the facilities long enough to take a bath. After a while I heard the bathroom door open, and then she wandered around in my bedroom for a while. Finally she stuck a tousled head out around the edge of my bedroom door.

"Russell," she said in a moony voice, "I have wanted you so!"

I threw the crutch at her head. "You little scut, you were listening to the whole thing!"

She ducked the crutch. "Ah, and I was thrilled, it was *so* romantic. Tell me something, did you ever ask that babe if she wears falsies? They'd go with her personality."

I couldn't think of a retort any stronger than, 'Shut up,' so I changed the subject. "How the hell did you get back in here?" I asked her.

"You leave a spare set of keys around where they're easy to find," she said. "No kidding, you old werewolf, how did you happen to get a yen for a phoney like that?"

"I like the type."

"That physical type, no doubt you mean. You're not the kind to think about anything else in a woman, except availability. Well—I'm the same type."

"I saw her first."

"I'm the same type, and I'm a woman, not a combination of spaghetti accent and emotions dialled up like on a telephone."

"Elena doesn't hit people on the head with beer bottles."

"You threw a chair at me first. You need somebody to hit you back. You don't want that tinted, tainted witch. You want a woman like me! See!"

She swung the door wide. She'd taken a bath all right. She stood there in her smooth, shining tanned skin, the lights reflecting glistening highlights from the water at just the points you'd expect. There wasn't an ounce of surplus fat on her sleek, lusciously-curved body. She was clean, fresh and young. And it was eminently clear that her words—'Russell, I have wanted you so'—weren't merely mockery of Elena. They expressed what she felt too.

And me with a broken leg.

With a coldness far from typical of my inner mood, I said, "Go put on some clothes. You want to catch pneumonia?"

"I guess I might," she said scornfully. "From your icy breath, grandpaw."

"Don't be stupid. I've had a hard night, with no sleep—"

"I suppose you think it was cosy, snuggling in the closet with your overshoes."

"—and it's eight o'clock in the morning. Also, I've stepped in a gopher hole and busted my left leg. If I was ever in the mood for romantic dalliance—"

"You've been known to be!"

"—it wouldn't be now. You'll find pyjamas in the third drawer of the chest. Get into them."

She turned back into the bedroom and went slowly away from me. Her straight back was slim, and the rounded flare of her buttocks below showed no soft flesh. The muscles of her legs didn't ruin their shape; but the muscles were there. She was a girl in very good shape—physically. Mentally, she was riding for a long fall.

I heard her get out the pyjamas. I heard the slap of linen as she turned back my bed. She raised her voice to call, "If you feel like staying there with your broken flipper, I'm sleeping here in your bed. I'm tired now."

"You might bring me a blanket."

She appeared with one. She looked small and lost in the great stiff folds of my pyjama coat—she hadn't bothered to put on the pants. Her black hair tangled down over the high wide collar, and her full breasts broke the straight fall of the floppy big jacket.

"Come here, kid."

She knelt down beside the chesterfield and I put my arms around her. She'd been rejected. She was tense and stiff to the touch.

"Stop messing around with me," I said harshly. "Sure, you'll get loved. But where does that put you in the end?"

"Do I look as if I had diamonds in my eyes? Am I the kind that expects to be staked to a fancy apartment, like that Italian bitch? I'll tell you. No."

"Then what the hell do you want?"

"I want *you*, you thin, scarred, sloppy wreck!" she said, and started to cry quietly. "I don't know what in heck it is you do to me, but I want to look after you. Believe me, it's the first time I ever wanted to look after anyone but Lila."

"Ah, the old game of lahv," I said in some disgust. "No doubt there are guys who want you. And you want me, and I want Elena, and Elena wants—"

"A bank account."

"Okay, you've cured me," I said. "An illusion will only stand so much ridicule. If you're trying to cut her out, she's cut. Now lay off her."

For answer, she kissed me affectionately.

"But I warn you—"

"You can't warn me against anything, wolf-boy. I started through the mill when I was fifteen and ran away from my folks. The millstones have pounded all necessary information into me."

"Well, you've put yourself in a position. The position is, you'll stick around for a while and eventually get kicked out. I want no bitter tears, and like they say no recriminations, when that happens."

"Maybe I'll leave first," she said pertly. "Move over, that couch is wide enough for two."

"I've got a broken leg!" I objected.

"All I want is a nice, cosy sleep. Give me half that blanket!"

Chapter Eighteen

I LAY IN THAT DELICIOUS half-consciousness between sleep and the grind of waking life, the warmth of Lila's body snuggling beside me, and my thoughts played idly and drowsily over past events.

I did not think of the case. At few times have I cared less who ever murdered whom. I thought about women. I do not boast when I say there were a lot of women to think about.

I will write a book, I mused, about Women I Have Known. Not women I have loved, certainly, nor even women I have slept with. Just women I have known. Like, a brunette named Pamela who had been incredibly beautiful, wonderful to love, and a crazy murderess. A big, sunny blonde named Inez who had given her love to a crooked chiseller, and got in jail because they thought she murdered him, and never succeeded in picking up much interest in life again even with most of the money in the city at her disposal. A cheap little blonde called Carol whose love was a commodity, not too high-priced, and whose pay for a last burst of affection was a fatal bullet.

Then an airline stewardess, name of Maida Malone—Maida with the sea-green eyes, the figure no dress could possibly make shapeless, who had a nervous collapse after she was almost arrested for murder. And Ann—the redhead with bands on her teeth—no kidding, bands!—the girl I somehow kept thinking I might marry. The only girl I'd ever thought about settling down with . . . someday.

And now, this case; and who did we have? Elena, the dream of beauty. Something I'd wanted the way a kid wants an expensive toy. To play with, and probably to break and throw away. I didn't think there was much more than that to it. Sure, she was lovely and she knew how to fix car engines. Aside from that she was a weak, backboneless gal who took the easy way every time—I thought. The dream died a little hard, but it was dying.

There entered also Priscilla, a little girl who loved skiing, a girl I could probably learn to love like a brother—but like a brother, period.

And Lila. What can you do in self-defence when a woman comes into your life by hitting you over the head with a beer bottle—and then decides to stay around? I looked at her. She was sleeping on her side with her face on her hands, her mouth parted and the long lashes of her closed eyes resting on her cheeks. I didn't know where she'd come from, what she'd been through, what men had known her, what she wanted out of life, what—hell, let's just say I didn't know her. And I was damned certain she didn't know me. But she wanted to stick around me for a while; just from what showed on the surface, she felt some hidden appeal from me. I liked her. I'd let her stick all right.

Because somehow she suddenly made Ann's approach to me seem dull, dead and cold—yeah, Ann, the beautiful redhead. The girl who had a house in the suburbs and the five children in her eyes. That was all right, but maybe I just wasn't mature. It didn't seem to me I was old enough for that yet.

So I mused until the front door clicked open and before I felt like moving or anything, Framboise was standing there—clearing his throat again. It was getting to be a bad habit with him.

"Hi beg your pardon," he said politely.

"Hi beg your pardon, too," I said. "There's no beer on

the ice. You'll have to drink rye, it's in the kitchen. Don't think anything of this. She's my sister."

"Ho, now hi didn't t'ink anyt'ing so bad as t'at," Framboise said, leering.

"What a mind you've got," I grunted. I dug my elbow gently in Delilah's ribs, several times, with no effect. She muttered a few unintelligible curses and slept on.

"Lila!" I said. All I got was a snort. I told Framboise, "You're a big, strong boy. And I've got a broken leg. You lift her off here while I get out."

Framboise picked Lila up. He had a few instincts of a gentleman because he was careful to pick her up the blanket with her and keep it over her. I rolled off the chesterfield and he put her back. She growled, like a dog chasing a cat in its sleep, but she didn't wake up.

Danny Moore had mounted a metal hoop in the bottom of the cast. I was supposed to be able to walk on it when the plaster was good and dry. I crawled over to the wall, stood up, and kicked the cast tentatively against the nearest door frame. It gave back a dead, solid sound and felt rigid as a steel truss.

"I think I'm operational," I said. "Come on out to the kitchen. You can drink and I can eat. What time is it?"

"Four-t'irty."

"Oh, fine. I was supposed to have a conference with MacArnold and Montgomery this morning."

I went to the phone, which I had thoughtfully unplugged early in the morning before retiring. I plugged it in, and it immediately started to ring. I looked at it, trying to gather strength. Then I unplugged it again.

"Coffee," I told Framboise. "Then I can face what's left of the day. What are you doing back here?"

"I tol' you I would come back. I couldn' sleep, not since

noon. I 'ave brought together a t'eory."

"Well, get ready to amend it. You left this morning before you heard the full story."

"*Comment?*"

"How d'you think I got this broken leg? Playing hop scotch with the neighborhood kids? I got one small thing in return for this disability here. I established a link between Crawfie Foster and Irish Joe. The way it went before, either Crawfie was talking the pictures as a private blackmailing enterprise of his own—which was possible—or he and Irish Joe were in it together. I caught up with Crawfie last night—at last. I followed him to a meeting-place where Irish Joe and the Indian talked to him. Then they saw me. They didn't bother to talk to me. They just jumped me."

"Ho," he said.

"So now what have we got? Foster and Irish Joe co-operating to shoot pictures that aren't good for anything but blackmail, and yet aren't used for that."

"Exactly where my theory comes in. You know w'at else t'e pictures could be used for? Identification."

"That's a big word," I said. "Just what the hell does it mean—in this connection?"

"T'is third partner. 'E is very anxious to keep out of t'e picture, no? Say 'e has a grudge against Wales. 'E knows Wales is a customer of t'e gambling joint. So 'e arranges wit' Irish Joe to have pictures of all t'e customers snapped. Irish Joe employs Crawfie for t'is purpose. Now, 'e doesn't even 'ave to appear near the gambling joint to identify Wales. 'E identifies 'im from a picture. 'E puts a finger on 'im an' the nex' time Wales comes to gamble, Bingo."

"Yeah?" I said. I guess I sounded cynical.

"Hokay, it's only an idea. It doesn't hexplain much, an' we have to find out a lot to prove it. But it's an idea to work from. An' if t'ere is no blackmail, 'ow else do you explain t'e pictures?"

I mulled it over. "Pictures for blackmail, no," I mused. "So pictures—for identification? Could be. Maybe you haven't got the rest of it right, but that might be a place to start. I'll work it over. What are you going to do?"

"Go furt'er into Wales' background."

"How about trying to locate the third partner?"

"Ah," he said smoothly, "but you and your friends are t'e ones wit' the confidential information. W'y don't you fin' out?"

"I'll try," I said grimly, "hard. Meanwhile, when do your boys get smart enough to find where Foster and Irish Joe are hiding?"

Framboise grunted disgustedly. "T'e skip-tracers 'ave been working on Foster since 'e disappeared—t'ere was a complaint t'en. My boys 'ave joined t'e search since you said 'e mebbe shot t'e Dover girl. But 'e has sure disappeared. An' as for Irish Joe, we are jus' getting hon 'is trail. We didn' know t'e owner of t'at gambling place until you tol' me earlier today. Now we 'ave a description out on 'im. An' on 'is Indian friend. We'll fin' t'em."

"When you bring them in, let me know. I want to come down and jump on their legs."

The front door started to quake as though at least six people were hammering on it at once. Framboise raised an eyebrow.

"MacArnold, probably," I explained.

" 'E mus' have been in bed early las' night. 'E is very strong t'is afternoon."

I got painfully to my feet, or rather to my foot and my cast. Framboise said, "Never mind. I'll let 'im in. I'm going in any case."

"Okay. Phone me if you get anything."

"Please, in the name of the *Sacré Coeur*, do the same for me," he said, and left.

From the hallway I heard MacArnold introducing Framboise to Montgomery. There was a brief silence and then Framboise in his deep voice said, "I t'ink I've seen you before, have I not, M'sieu?"

Montgomery said drily, "Sure. You helped arrest me the other night."

"Oh?"

"I was gambling on an unfortunate evening. Besides, I was the one who found Chesterley's body. Remember?"

"Ho, *oui*, T'at is your interest in t'is case."

"That was the beginning of my interest," Montgomery said. "But only the beginning."

Then Framboise slammed the door behind him and MacArnold and Montgomery came out to the kitchen. They looked at my cast. They said simultaneously, "Well, for the love of God!" and "What the hell did you do to yourself?"

"Just a skiing accident," I said casually.

"Yeah. In June."

"All right, so I slipped in the bath tub."

"You are not funny," MacArnold informed me, "and we've been trying to rouse you since ten a.m. Come on, what's up?"

I told him the whole story.

"Well, that's fine," said MacArnold scornfully. "You can really fluff things up. You locate Crawfie and let him slip away. You let Irish Joe and the Indian get away too. You don't even get your car back."

"Okay, rub it in," I said. "What bright accomplishments have you and Montgomery performed?"

"We built ourselves up two fine hangovers in Louis

Two's," Montgomery said. "Period."

"Okay. At least I established that Crawfie and Irish Joe are working together."

"Yeah, but where does that leave us on our list of problems?" Montgomery dragged a sheet of paper from his pocket and unfolded it, and we all looked:

1. Can we prove Irish Joe and the Indian killed Chesterley?

"No," I said, "not unless we beat a confession out of them. But it's still as good a guess as any."

2. Where is Crawfie Foster?

"Teed's established he's still in the city," said Mac, "and we still have to pin him down."

3. How were the pictures taken?

4. Who shot Priscilla Dover?

5. Why aren't the pictures being used for blackmail?

There was nothing new on three and four, so no comments were made. About five I said, "Framboise has a somewhat screwy idea. He thinks the shots were taken to identify Wales for someone—say the third partner—who didn't dare show up at apartment sixteen. This guy put the finger on Wales' pic, and Wales was rubbed out."

"Ah, how far-fetched can you get?" Montgomery asked.

"They aren't being used for blackmail," I maintained.

"I'll bet they aren't being used for that either. Let's admit a blank on that one and carry on."

6. Why was Wales killed?

"And who killed him?" Mac wanted to know. "I don't get that one at all."

"Nobody does," I grouched. "Go on."

7. How did Priscilla find out about the pictures?

Montgomery said, "If we knew that, I'll bet we'd know where Crawfie's hideout is. She must have followed him to it. When will she be able to talk?"

"Finish the list, and I'll ask Danny Moore," I said. "When I talked to him last night in the hospital he said she was coming along well. Still weak, but recovering."

8. Are Irish Joe and Crawfie working together?

"I answered that," I said, and rubbed it in, "even if it was supposed to be MacArnold's problem.

"Better you should have solved your own problem."

9. Who is the third partner in the gambling house?

MacArnold turned to Montgomery. "All right, sound off. That was your line of enquiry. Did you find out who it was, or do you still think it was one of us?"

"I'll sketch in the requirements for the third partner," said Montgomery. "He either agreed to, or assisted in the Chesterley killing; that could be anybody. He knew Teed was interested in the case and had Irish Joe beat him up—that could be MacArnold or me. He knew Priscilla had discovered Crawfie's secret, and that could by myself or Teed. He shot Priscilla—that could be anybody, including Teed, because none of us have alibis for the time it happened. He probably shot Wales. That lets out you and MacArnold, Teed, but it doesn't let me out unless you want to take my word I'm not the guy."

"I guess we can take your word. Anyway, we don't need to make it so personal. It doesn't *have* to be one of us, you know. It could be just the little Indian. It might be Crawfie. It might have been Wales because perhaps Wales was shot to increase Irish Joe's profits—if he was the third partner."

"In other words, it might have been almost anybody," MacArnold decided. "The tenth item is, 'Why was the Riley stolen?' That's not a vital question, so I guess we've completed the review."

"It's vital enough," I roared. "However, I'm beginning to

think they just took it because I was out of commission and that made it easy to steal. They wanted a good car to use."

"Now what do we do?"

"I go to the can," Montgomery said. He came back in a minute dangling an intimate item of female dress from one finger—a rather translucent pair of white nylon briefs.

"What's this? Souvenir of one that got away?"

"Oh, hell. I forgot about Lila. Go wake her up, will you?" I asked him. "She's on the chesterfield."

"Better just leave her there for when you come in tonight," MacArnold suggested.

"I don't like your evil minds. Get out."

"What are you going to do?"

"Go up to the hospital to see Priscilla. I'm sure it won't hurt her to talk for a few minutes, and it's getting pretty vital to have her information. Wales had been added to the death list. Maybe there'll be more, unless we clean this up. Somebody's playing for enough chips to take human life awful easily."

"Okay, what'll we do?" Montgomery asked.

"Anything you can think of. I haven't got any other ideas. If you don't get hot on a trail, stay near a phone. I'll ring you if I get anything from Priscilla."

"We'll go to my place," MacArnold decided. "My beer-well hasn't been drawn on much lately."

They left together. I stumped into the front room and shook Lila. "Okay, kid, enough sack-time," I said. "I got a use for you."

She turned over and opened her eyes lazily. "I was beginning to think you'd never find one," she said. "What was all the commotion?"

"Three guys have come and gone. We're trying to solve a murder case, or did you know?"

"Seems to me I've heard about it." She got off the chesterfield, modestly pulling the pyjama jacket down over her round thighs. There was a small amount of hell to pay when she couldn't find her pants in the bathroom, but aside from that she dressed uneventfully, swilled down half a tin of grapefruit juice and a cup of coffee, and we went out to the Morris. She drove it well, which was a good thing. I was in no condition to drive a car.

We stopped at a florist's and got an armful of red roses. Then we crawled up the hill to the hospital. They told me at the desk Priscilla was in the private patients' pavilion, on the fifth floor. For two bucks I took a load off my cast, and got the porter to settle me in a wheelchair and get me to the general region of Priscilla's room.

The floor nurse was behind a desk in a small glassed-in cubicle. "How's Miss Dover today?" I asked her.

"She's done remarkably well," the nurse told me. She reached for a folder containing charts, and flipped over them. "She had a good rest last night, and she's been eating well today. Of course she's very weak. No visitors."

"I'm the next of kin."

"Oh—you're Mr. Dover—her father?"

"No, I'm just her sponsor here. But I'm the nearest thing she's got in this city. May I see her?"

"I suppose so. Go down and peek in her door. I wouldn't go in if she's asleep."

I hobbled self-consciously down the hall, trying not to make noise with my steel-shod stump. I came to Priscilla's room and pushed open the door. I needn't have worried. The rooms were soundproofed by a second heavy door on the inside.

I eased open the sluggish, silent door. Her window blind was up and the room was bright. Priscilla lay in the bed asleep.

She looked very small and frail in the hospital bed. Her face had scarcely more color than the sheets. They'd pulled her long brown hair up in a severe, tight coiffure, leaving her ears and thin little neck naked, somehow indecent.

Then I saw the blue bruises at her neck.

For a minute I forgot I had a broken leg. I tried to run toward her and my cast tangled with the half-open door. I went flat on my face with a crash that knocked out my wind and was about hard enough to crack the plaster on my leg. But I didn't stop to see what damage had been done. I kept on toward her, first crawling, then staggering erect.

At the bedside I felt for her pulse, and finding nothing listened for her heart. I listened for minutes.

I heard nothing. This time, I'd been too late.

I hobbled back to the door and yelled, "Nurse!"

The floor nurse came toward me with a machine-gun clacking of leather heels. "Please! We must have quiet—"

"Get an interne. Fast!"

She didn't argue. She turned and ran quickly, with a swish of her starched skirts, back to her cubicle.

I went into Priscilla's room again, and it began to hit me. There was nothing I could do. I'd been powerless to catch the bastards who did this. I'd worked too slowly, been too stupid, failed and failed and failed.

Rage came over me in a rush. My fingers itched for a gun, or for the feel of an evil throat under them. I wanted to shoot, to choke, to smash, to kill.

They talk about eradicating war. Hell, there will be wars long after people stop having babies. Hate is stronger than love; it's stronger than anything. The foulness of this crime appalled me. But it didn't make me want to retire from the world and be a Trappist monk.

It made me want to kill.

The interne and the nurse came in together. The interne was tall, dark, square-faced. He was going to make a good doctor; already he had the quiet manner that handles emergencies without so much as a raised voice. As he reached the bed he said quickly but calmly to the nurse, "Emergency surgical wagon. Hurry it."

She swished out. He lifted Priscilla's eyelids, lowered them again, shook his head. He stripped back the bed covers, and pulled away the hospital gown to bare her breast. He lifted his stethoscope and listened.

The nurse brought in a white enamel, rubber-tired wagon with bottled drugs and surgical instruments laid out, ready for use, under a sterile cloth which she whisked aside. She looked questioningly at him. "Long needle? Adrenalin?"

He shook his head. He replaced Priscilla's gown and lifted the bed clothes gently, up—and over her face.

"I'm sorry," he told me. "I'm afraid I'll have to detain you. Would you tell me what happened?"

"I found her like this. I called the nurse."

"She has been strangled."

The nurse drew her breath in sharply and covered her mouth.

"Who else had been here to her, nurse?"

"No one, doctor. She's not allowed visitors.

"Could anyone get in here?" I asked.

"Not without passing my cubicle. And of course, I make sure I know the business of anyone who comes to this floor."

"Are you ever out of the cubicle?"

"There is a second nurse on the floor. One of us is always there."

The interne shook his head. "There is a staircase at the end of the corridor. Anyone could come up that way and reach this room without being seen. But—I'm afraid you'd better stay until we get the police, Mr.—?"

"Teed. I'll be glad to stay. When you call Homicide, will you ask them to send Detective-Sergeant Framboise? He knows this case."

"I will," the interne said gravely.

"I'd like to speak to him too."

"All right. Come with me."

We left the nurse with Priscilla and went to the cubicle. When Framboise came on the line and the interne had reported to him, I took the phone. "I've got to get to work. Will you tell this doctor to tell me to go?"

"Sure. Don't do ant'ing foolish."

"I wish to God I could. But I don't even know where I can lay my hands on any of them."

He talked to the interne again, and the interne nodded. I was free to leave. But first, there was one thing I had to do. Somehow, I hated to do it. I called MacArnold's number.

"Hi," I said. "Montgomery with you?"

"Why, no," Mac said. "He dropped me off here. Then he decided to go back to his own place for a while."

I hung up before he could ask me what was wrong.

Chapter Nineteen

THE MORRIS WAS PARKED just beside the front door of the private patients' pavilion. I got awkwardly into the seat beside Lila.

"You look a bit rocky," she said. "Leg hurt?"

"No. Let's go"

"I bet I know what's wrong. You haven't had a drink since eight this morning."

"Oh, shut up. Start that car."

"My God, has someone just told you you have cancer? What's wrong?"

"Don't be so damn flip. Come on, I want to get back to the apartment."

"All right." We went down the driveway and along Pine and Cedar to Cote des Neiges.

She said, "Maybe I forced myself on you. That doesn't mean I'll sit around like a little puppy, waiting to be kicked. If you could drive this car I'd leave you here."

"Sorry. Priscilla's dead."

"Oh. Oh, gee. I thought she was getting better."

"She was a lot better until some bastard crept into her hospital room and throttled her."

"Oh, no!"

"Yeah. Here we are. You got your key to my place?"

"Yes."

"Go up and get my gun and holster. In the hall closet. Then look in the top drawer of the desk in the living room and bring a box of shells from there."

When she came back I buckled the holster under my arm. I loaded the gun, filled an extra clip with shells and put it in my pocket. “All right, down to Sherbrooke Street,” I said.

We stopped in front of the apartment building where Irish Joe had operated his business; where Paul Hanwood lived his useless life; where Wales had lost his. For the first time, I was coming in there with business really on my mind.

I got off the elevator at the eighth floor. The cops had put a padlock on the door of apartment sixteen. The padlock held together the ends of a chain that ran through heavy steel dogs set into the door and the frame. I could blow the chain apart with a shot, but if someone was inside I didn’t want to warn them I was coming.

Few padlocks are difficult, and this was a standard model. I took a tempered steel probe from my pocket, put it into the keyhole of the padlock, and picked. The catches didn’t release right away, but the body of the lock was soft sheet steel. I levered it out of shape with shaft of the probe, gave myself room to work, and had the thing unhitched in one minute. The chain slipped away. The door wasn’t locked.

Framboise was going to be mad at me, but I was in.

I drew my gun and padded with one foot, thumped with the cast through the darkened entryway. The place was still as a crematorium at night.

The buffet-bar room was empty. The padded door to the gambling room had been smashed off its hinges, probably by the vice squad when they made their raid. I went on. The gaming room was a wreck. Roulette wheels had been smashed, the green baize on the crap tables was torn. Chips were strewn on the floor. I picked my way through the mess.

I came to the door at the side of the room, giving on the corridor that led to Irish Joe’s office—the corridor I’d started down before, only to have the little Indian recognize me before I could complete my trip. I opened the door, and there was complete darkness inside.

I felt my way down the corridor, I was making too much noise, with my steel foot, and I didn't feel happy about that. On the other hand if anyone wanted a gun fight, I was really in the mood for one. I figured to be cautious enough so nobody would jump me before my gun could talk to him.

At the end of the corridor, the door to Irish Joe's office was ajar. Light came through the crack, meaning there was at least a window in the office to let me see where I was. I reached out with the gun muzzle and nudged the door. It swung quietly open.

Irish Joe had done himself proud here. The carpeting was heavy, and wall-to-wall. There was a massive mahogany desk in the middle of the room, with matching chairs placed around it. On the far side of the room, under the window, was a richly-upholstered couch. Somebody was asleep on it.

I froze, but the guy hadn't heard me. He didn't stir.

It was the little sheep-dog who'd guarded the front door of the apartment. He had a few days' growth of black beard on his ugly puss. He was still wearing evening clothes, but they looked as though he'd been greasing cars in them.

I came close to him. One hand flopped down over the side of the couch. I brought my gun up and down hard, and I left a scar on the hand that would take a while to heal.

He jumped, and whimpered almost before he was awake. He drew his arms and legs up, protecting his body, and his cut hand dragged across the lapel of his coat as he raised it. That made him wince and cry out, and his eyes stared open at me.

"Where is everybody?" I asked him.

"Jeez, Mac, lay off. Watcha doing here?"

"Looking for Irish Joe," I said. I took the safety off the

gun, slowly, making sure he saw me do it and heard the dirty little *click*. "Where's Irish Joe? Huh?"

"I don't know a thing," he said. "I got pinched when the place was raided. I just got outa the cooler this morning, and I come back here. I ain't seen anybody."

"How'd you get in?"

"Got a key to the back door."

"Who bailed you out of hoosegow?"

"Irish Joe's lawyer."

"All right. I want Irish Joe. Where should I look?"

"Jeez, I dunno. He lived here—before the raid. He ain't here now, but I dunno where he skipped to."

I brought the down and pointed the muzzle at his guts. "Get some ideas. Fast," I said.

"I don't know anythin'!" he screamed. "Jeez, he mighta skipped anywhere. How would I know?"

I shifted my grip on the gun and plowed up the side of his face with the butt. "Anything more you have to say, say it now!"

"Try—try apartment fifteen!" he yelled desperately.

"You're lying," I said. "I know who lives there."

He couldn't deny it. He couldn't answer me, he was shaking too hard.

"All right, I'll try. But you better wait here till I come back, so I can ask you some more if you're wrong."

I lifted the gun. He shrank back as far as he could go. His eyes were big. He screamed again. I could have hit him on the head to put him out, but I was fed up being nice to all these bastards. I clipped him just beside the eye, and heard the crunch of bone breaking. He went limp as a slice of raw liver. When the eye swelled up, he'd be easy to identify for quite a few days.

I cleared out of the place and went across the hall to

apartment fifteen. I rang the door bell, and waited, and rang it again. Nobody was home. Not to me, anyhow.

I got out the strip of celluloid and did my little trick with the lock on the door. It swung open. Inside everything was so quiet I could hear two clocks ticking in different rhythm, and away back in the kitchen a leaky faucet dripping slowly.

While I was there I looked at the door again. I tested its panels and examined them for tool-marks. They were solid, and nobody had monkeyed with them since the door was put together. God only knew how Crawfie could take pictures through the thing.

I went slowly and cautiously through the place, room by room, casing every nook, cranny and closet as I went and leaving all the doors open behind me. Hanwood's apartment could have been more luxurious. For instance, the walls could have been papered with gold leaf, and wall-to-wall mink might have looked good on the floors. Aside from that I had few suggestions to make. If he'd held an auction, he could have realized fifty thousand bucks without even taking the pictures off the walls. Selling them would have brought about a hundred grand more.

The place was incredible. The furniture was the kind an Earl of England would only sell to buy hospital space for his dying mother. The rugs must have been stolen from Eastern palaces—they were what the Persians keep for themselves, and never export. In the master bedroom was a four-poster George Washington never slept in—he wouldn't have been allowed to sit on it. All in all, there were enough furnishings to fill a twenty-room mansion, and then use it for a museum and sell tickets to the public at five dollars a head.

It was beautiful, if you liked that kind of thing. It was also completely empty. The little sheep-dog had been lying. I couldn't see any signs that Irish Joe had ever been here.

The guy had said the first thing that came into his head to keep from being slugged again.

I thought of going back to beat some more out of him. I decided that wasn't worthwhile because he didn't know anything. He'd been scared enough to blab if he had any idea where the other boys were.

I hobbled out, slammed Hanwood's door behind me, and took the elevator down. When I got to the Morris, Lila said, "Get anything?"

"No. Anything happen here?"

"No. Oh, a man gave the Morris a funny look, a minute ago. He went past on the sidewalk and turned into the apartment building. You didn't pass him coming out?"

"No. What did he look like?"

"Nothing out of the ordinary. He was well-dressed, about your height. Good looking."

"Dark hair?"

"Had a hat on."

"Could have been Hanwood," I said. "Too bad I missed him, but it couldn't matter less. I guess we might as well go back to my place."

"No more ideas?"

"Not right now."

We were silent on the trip back up Cote des Neiges to my apartment. I was thinking. Thinking didn't get me anywhere.

When we got in, she said, "Want me to mix you a drink?"

"I don't feel like anything. You go ahead, if you want."

She went to the kitchen. I noticed the phone was still unplugged, and idly plugged it in. It was quiet for a minute, and then as usual began to ring.

"Hello," I said. "Yes, this is Teed."

When he first said it I could hardly believe my ears. I

sat down on the chair in the entry and made him repeat it. "You *what?*"

Hamish MacFaden cleared his throat. "You were right, Mr. Teed, after all. I'm being blackmailed."

"Thank God."

"I don't feel exactly that way about it," he said waspishly.

"It may help to clean up three murders," I told him. "What's happened?"

"I got a copy of that picture in the mail today—the one you showed me. With it was a typed note asking for ten thousand."

I whistled. "They play high. I didn't think it would be that much."

MacFaden said with regret in his voice, "I'm afraid they've gauged it pretty well, Mr. Teed. They threaten to send this picture to the newspapers, along with a detailed record of every time I stepped into that place, how long I stayed, how much I lost or won. The papers would print that, of course, because the picture authenticates it. And I couldn't sue because it would be true. So it's worth ten thousand to avoid exposure."

"You realize that would be just a first instalment."

"Of course. At the same time, it is a question of money loss rather than the complete ruination of my life. Can you imagine how long a bank president would last, if it were known that he gambled illegally—in a place so disreputable a man has been killed there?"

"I see what you mean. But how long can you go on paying out ten-grand sums?"

"I propose to pay not ten, but twenty, immediately. Ten will go to them to keep them quiet temporarily. The other ten is in the mail addressed to you. I presume from what you said before that you want to catch these men. Regard the money from me as a retainer, and please devote your entire efforts to catching them."

"I already am. But I have a hunch this development may help me. What are the details of payment?"

"They want me to get the money in small bills."

"Yes, yes, but where do you take it?"

He hesitated.

"MacFaden, for God's sake don't get coy," I said. "If I can meet the blackmailers at the place you're supposed to leave the money, they won't send any pictures to any newspapers. They won't even talk to anybody ever again. If I miss them, they'll never know. I'll be careful, I promise you."

"All right," he said. "You can do what you wish. But I propose to follow the instructions to the letter, and leave the money at the proper place. I drew it out of the bank before closing."

"Fine. Where and when?"

There was the rustle of paper as he consulted the note he's been sent. "I am to go to the corner of Decarie Boulevard and Cote de Liesse Road. I go completely around the traffic circle, come back Decarie about one hundred yards, and stop the car. Then I get out and walk across Decarie—that all seems very elaborate, doesn't it? Why do I double back?"

"Do just what they say," I advised him. "It's so they can spot you and make sure you're alone, and not being followed by cops."

"There's supposed to be a deserted roadside canteen just there. I am to go behind the canteen and leave the money on the ground just at its back door. The money is to be wrapped in a large white-paper package so it will be easy to find. I am to do all this at exactly midnight."

"Fine. You do it. About eleven o'clock I'll approach the

hut from another direction and hide out. I don't expect they'll be there until after you leave the money—they'll stay concealed somewhere and watch you come and go. But in any case I won't start anything until you've left."

"All right. Be careful."

"I will. I'll call you as soon as I can and tell you what happens."

He hung up. I looked at my watch. It was nine o'clock. I had almost two hours to wait before doing anything. I should have phoned MacArnold to tell him of Priscilla's death, but I couldn't face talking about that yet. I went into the kitchen, pulled out some supplies and started making dinner to keep myself from drinking. I wanted a very steady hand for later on.

When I was through with inch-thick lamb chops rubbed over lightly with garlic, seared in a pan and then grilled under a red hot flame until they were almost black outside and tender as chicken inside, I loaded everything on a tray and got Lila to carry it to the living room. I sat down on the floor to eat. It was the most comfortable way to support the cast.

Lila worked very slowly through about one-third of her chop and then pushed it away.

"What's wrong with my cooking?" I demanded.

"Listen, dammit, are you going out there tonight and get yourself shot up?"

"Oh, no. I'm the guy who's doing the shooting. I've got surprise on my side. You want to worry about something, worry about the time I parachuted into occupied France and landed plunk on the tin roof of a German barracks."

"You got out of that one," she said. "That's past. This is in the future."

I pulled her over my knees and kissed her on the nose. "It'll be past by morning," I said. "And I've got a suspicion we'll be able to relax and enjoy life then. You ever seen Bermuda? There's a ten-grand cheque on its way to me in the mails."

"Send it back," she said, "and stay home tonight."

I didn't bother to argue. What you have to do, you have to do. I was silent for a while, and she slowly stopped fretting. I was turning things over in my mind.

Later I pulled the two shots again out of my pocket—the shot of Hamish, and the one of the late investment banker, Wales. I studied them. I handed them to Lila.

"Look at those again. Notice anything more?"

"No. Should I?"

"You said last time you had the uneasy idea something was screwy about them. Has it struck you? I went back to that place this afternoon and inspected it again, and I don't see how those shots were taken. So help me, nobody should shoot through an oak door."

"So?"

"Let me see them again."

I looked at them for a while longer. "They couldn't be fakes, could they?"

"Why should they be fakes? I mean, there's no reason why they couldn't be real. Those guys actually did step through that door, at one time or another, didn't they?"

"Yes. But when they were stepping through they would be looking right at the camera. They couldn't help seeing it. Yet they never knew the shots were taken. So maybe—"

"Maybe is right!" She leaned against my shoulder and pointed. "The door is in exactly the same position in both shots. And the lighting on the door—that's what was screwy! The door is lit exactly the same way in both shots. But the light falls on the faces from the left in this one, and from the right in the other. Sure. Fakes!"

"How was it done?"

"Got a magnifying glass?"

"Yes, look in the desk drawer."

She came back with it and studied them some more. She said, "It's one hell of an expert job. I don't see any obvious signs the negative's been tampered with. But probably the photographer took one shot of the door, and made prints of it. Then he started shooting these guys. In each case, he makes a print, cuts it out around the edge of the figure, and pastes it into one print of the doorway. Then he retouches to make it look okay, and re-photographs the montage. This is a print from that new negative."

"The perfect way to work the gag!" I said. "Since these guys had all actually been in that apartment, they'd never think of calling the shot a fake."

"Where does all this get you?"

"It tells me," I said slowly, trying to think ahead, "that I've got to look someplace very special for Crawfie Foster. Someplace where he could hide and shoot a lot of big financial boys."

Chapter Twenty

I LOOKED AT THE CLOCK. "Ten-thirty," I said.

"You want me to drive you to this place?"

"I can't drive myself, and I'm damn well not going to walk," I snapped.

"You're getting jumpy. Calm down."

"Sure. It's just the big build-up. I've been waiting so long to get my hands on these lugs, I can hardly stand to wait any longer."

"Anything you want me to do?"

I thought. "Yes. I'm going to need the flashlight badly, and they might get away if it goes on the bum. Take the Morris and hunt up someplace where you buy really fresh batteries for it."

"At this time of night?"

"You asked if there was anything you could do."

"Okay. Maybe drug stores carry them." She went out.

I was nervous all right. I pulled my gun from its holster and unloaded and loaded it again. I remembered something. I went to the desk and took Paul Hanwood's automatic from the drawer where I'd hidden it after knocking it out of his hand. He didn't know how to keep a gun in very good shape. I got oil and a rag in the kitchen and cleaned it up. I checked it and made sure it had a full load too.

Lila should be back waiting downstairs by now. I stumped to the door, turned off the lights, and opened it.

Paul Hanwood was waiting just in front of the door. He'd found himself a new gun. He was pointing it at my gut.

"I was about to ring," he said politely. "But I heard you coming to the door. Shall we go back inside?"

"No. Shoot me here, if you want to."

"Please don't tempt me. You may recall you called my bluff once before. Do I have to do what I did that time?"

I grinned. "Try it."

He looked at me steadily. "Teed, I'm not the careless, gun-packing type you're used to. I don't pull a gun on all tight occasions, as I imagine you do. When I take one in my hand, it's because I expect to use it. Now, shall I shoot? I advise you to go back inside. And don't try slamming the door in my face; I'll shoot through it."

You know something? He wasn't kidding. Whatever was under his skin would drive him right straight to murder if he didn't get his own way.

I backed into the apartment. I turned the lights back on. He came in after me and closed the door.

"Keep going," he said. "Your living room will do."

This time he kept his distance behind me. He wasn't going to have this gun knocked out of his hand. And I didn't dare reach for either of mine—he was too tense to take chances with.

In the living room I faced him again. He was keeping his distance still. He was watching every move I made. And I didn't like the wildness in his eyes.

"Teed," he said hoarsely, "you're going to die. First, I want to tell you why."

"Thoughtful of you," I said. I tried to make up my mind which gun to reach for—the one in the shoulder holster, or the one in my jacket pocket.

"You searched my apartment today!" He accused me.

"Now, that's a good reason for killing me," I said. "A very good reason. With that one, you could plead insanity and get away with it."

"I don't intend to plead anything. You're in the middle

of a case at the moment. If you are shot, the police won't find suspects lacking. And that means they're not likely to think of me."

"Got it all figured out, haven't you?"

"I have indeed. I have it so well figured that you should be dead, and Elena back with me, by tonight."

"So that's it?"

"She spent the night with you last night, Teed!"

"Yeah. In a hospital."

"I don't care what you did. The important thing is, she has left me. This morning when I went to her apartment, she had moved out. I don't even know where she's gone. But I want her back, Teed, more than anything else in the world. And she'll come back, she'll have to come back when you're dead."

"Good theory. Might not work out."

"We'll see. At any rate, I'll have the satisfaction of killing you."

"Yeah?" I reached quickly for the jacket-pocket gun.

Quickly, I said. Not quickly enough. His gun went off and spat out a bullet that, luckily, went right through the cloth of the jacket between my hand and my side.

It discouraged me. I stood with my hands out from my sides, motionless as a side of beef in the deep-freezer.

Then came a thunderous pounding on the door.

"Well, well," I said. "You stalled too long. Put your gun away. There's no back door to this apartment."

He grinned. "There is. I happen to know."

"Those are cops," I said. "I was waiting here for them when you came to the door. One more shot from that gun of yours, and they'll be swarming into this place before you can move.

"All is not yet lost. I hate bloodshed. You let me go, and

I'll take them away with me. You can leave here later and I'll forget the whole thing. Also you can have Elena back—if she'll come. I have other interests."

"You're giving up easily."

"I'm making a bargain. It's a good one for me. It's a good one for you too."

He put his gun away.

"Wait here till the coast is clear," I said.

I walked through the entry and out of the apartment. I closed the door quickly after me because it wasn't the police doing the hammering.

It was Mrs. MacEchran. And was she mad!

"You!" she screamed. "You—you shooting gallery!"

I took her prune-like old face between my hands, brushing some of the stringy red hair out of my way. Then I kissed her gently on the forehead. "God bless you, mother!" I said fervently. I walked away before she could decide to faint.

Chapter Twenty-One

"YOU'LL HAVE TO TAKE A CHANCE on the flashlight," Lila said crossly. "I looked all over hell, and couldn't find any place that sold batteries at night."

"Fine," I said pleasantly.

"You seem more relaxed."

"Fine night for a murder." I looked up at the sky. It was clouded over, and not a star was visible.

"Oh, sure. Couldn't be better."

"Turn this way," I said. "We go out through the Town of Mount Royal. I don't want us cruising along Decarie, where they might spot us. Boy, this is going to be a pipe."

"You're so sure?"

"Listen, I just spent ten minutes looking down a gun-muzzle. A maniac thought he wanted to kill me. I got away from him. My life is charmed, kid."

"Mother of Heaven!" she swore. "I can't leave you alone to go to the drug store. Who was it this time?"

"Hanwood. Elena's boy friend. He's relatively harmless."

"Sure. He just wanted to kill you. He won't for much longer. You can tell the bitch that I'll shave off all her hair if she shows in your apartment once more."

"Ah, ah, ah!" I said reprovingly.

"What did you do with Hanwood?"

"Left him in the apartment."

"Oh, fine. What do we do, buy a couple of butterfly nets so we can catch him when we get back?"

"He'll be gone by then. After this is over I'll have a little talk with him, and if he's still unreasonable I'll give him to the men with the straight jackets."

We were in the middle of the Town of Mount Royal. "Now where do I go?" she wanted to know.

"Turn here, around the circle, and then turn left onto Graham Boulevard. That'll bring us back out toward the corner of Decarie and Cote de Liesse. I'm going to scramble through a few fields."

"With your broken leg?"

"This broken leg," I said, "is going back where it was broken to beat the breakers over the head."

We went on for a while. The prim little new houses of the Town petered out and we drove through open fields. I said, "Okay. This'll do," and Lila stopped the car.

I got out. She got out.

"Where do you think you're going?" I asked.

"I'm coming to see the show."

"Like hell you are. Get back in the car."

"You were just saying what a pipe it would be. Remember? Nobody stood a chance of getting hurt. Okay, I'll come."

"Listen, there's going to be shooting. Don't kid yourself on that score. I'll be able to look after myself, but I don't want you to worry about."

She got stubborn. "If it's too dangerous for me, it's too dangerous for you. Either I go, or you don't go."

I limped over to her and put my hands on her shoulders. "Kid, this is my business. Not yours. I saw pictures of the way Chesterley was beaten, up on the mountain. I found Priscilla bleeding to death after she was shot. I looked into the glassy eyes of this guy Wales just after he was killed. Now, today, I found Priscilla laying there in the hospital, strangled—a sick, helpless kid, recovering from a trip down to the last step before the door to death, strangled in her hospital bed! A swell, right-minded kid who never did wrong in her life.

You know how I feel?"

I stopped for breath. I looked into her face for some effect of my words. She was affected.

"I feel this way. I want to get my hands on that gang. I want to strangle them, shoot them, kick their guts out. And all this is my business—not yours. Get back in the car."

She got back in after that.

"So long," I said. "Wait right here. It might be as long as two hours. Catch some sleep if you feel like it. If this one manages to blow up, you may be chauffeuring all night."

"So long, Russ."

I set out across the fields.

Ever tramped across an over grown, once-plowed field on a dark and moonless night? Maybe you have; but have you ever tried it with one leg in a cast?

I trudged, stumbled, jarred my backbone every time the ground dipped away, and fell five times in the first ten minutes. I could have made as good time crawling on my belly.

Then I came to a barbed-wire fence. I tried putting my good leg over first, and couldn't get my cast over. I started again, heaved the cast over first, and its weight dragged my leg down on the wire. I tore my pants on the barbs, and cut my leg. I hauled the cast back and cursed considerable.

Lila said, just beside me, "I'll hold the wire up and you can crawl under it."

"What the hell are you doing here?"

"I thought you might have a little trouble."

"Well, this is the last fence. Hold the wire up and then get back to the car. If I catch you following me any more, so help me, I'll lay you out cold with this flashlight."

"Okay," she said. She sounded surly. She was sore. Fine. She got sore enough, she wouldn't care whether I got shot or not and I could do this on my own.

"And I mean it," I said. I hauled off and walloped her, hard, across the backside with the flashlight before I got down to crawl through the fence. She was so mad she almost dropped the wires on my back. I wouldn't have any more trouble with her.

I went on, in my stumbling fashion, across a second field. I hit another fence, but the strands were widely separated and I squeezed through without getting any major tears in my clothes.

And then, not too far away, I could see cars zooming by on Decarie. I went down on my hands and knees and crawled in the slow, easy, cautious way they taught us in the Infantry—each hand or knee touches the ground gently, and you ease weight down on it slowly. That way, not a sound; you don't even crack a twig.

After a little crawling I was close enough to the deserted canteen—it was fifteen yards away, as far as I could judge. I looked at the luminous dial of my wristwatch. Time had passed as I made my tortuous journey. It was nearly twelve.

I wondered where Irish Joe, or the Indian, or Crawfie Foster—whoever was to pick up the money—would be. They wouldn't be at the canteen, that was certain, in case Hamish MacFaden had decided to brave it out, tell the cops and bring them with him. But they also wouldn't be far away—they'd want to keep an eye on the money as soon as it passed from MacFaden's hands.

Before I had time to muse any more, I realized MacFaden was about to act his part in the play. A long, black car—it looked as though it might be a Caddy—drove slowly up Decarie past the canteen, circled the traffic circle and came back. It halted on the other side of the road. A very tall man got out of the car, waited for traffic to thin, then came across Decarie. The way I was lying, flat on the sod, his footsteps pounded dully at my ears as he came to the canteen.

I said a short prayer. I'd advised Hamish to carry this out. Surely to God they wouldn't be foolish enough to shoot him too!

I held my breath. But nothing happened. Hamish came to the back of the canteen and tossed a big, flat parcel on the grass—the light caught it just for an instant as it fell, and then you could barely see it lying in the shadow of the canteen. MacFaden turned and walked back to the road, and then across Decarie to his car. Everything was quiet again.

It was damp lying on the grass. And nothing was happening. The falling of the dew and the passing of cars on the street were all that went on. Until at last a car stopped, right in front of the canteen. I gritted my teeth in rage. It was a racy, low black roadster. It was Riley.

A man got out of the car. He wasn't more than twenty yards from me. He walked with mincing, nervous steps and kept glancing all around him. He was a fat little broad-bottomed duck in a hairy tweed jacket and shapeless pants.

He was Crawfie Foster. And he was all alone.

This was where we got Crawfie, ten thousand rocks, and the solution to all the crimes.

I got cautiously to my feet. He was between me and the light; I could see him, but he couldn't possibly see me. I moved noiselessly to the back of the canteen. I had to go slowly to avoid alarming him, but at that I was moving faster than he was. Almost dancing in his nervousness, he went forward a few steps, stopped, watched cars go past, darted back a step if a glimmer of reflected light chanced to touch him, then came on again. He looked like a startled faun in a ballet.

Whatever other merits his method of approach had, it allowed me to get good and ready for him. I stood well in the shadow of the canteen, so close to the package of money that when he bent over for it I could practically fall on his neck.

He came on. He saw the money. I held my breath. He still came on, which meant he sure as hell didn't see me.

It was all over fast. He got to the money and leaned over to get both hands on it. I took off, pulling my cast right along, and hit him solidly. I enveloped him. His wind came out with a choked scream, like the cry of a dying rabbit.

There never had been any fight in Crawfie Foster. There wasn't an ounce of resistance in his flabby body now, as I flipped him over on his back and sat on his stomach. The packet of dough was lying under his head like a pillow. I pulled it away and set it beside me, flopping his head in the dirt. Then I slapped his face. "Hi, Crawfie," I said. "It's Russ."

He didn't say anything. He probably couldn't.

"Your memory is no good. Years ago I told you what would happen if we ever met again." I slapped him some more. It made me feel good. I could have used the flashlight, or my gun, but I wanted to use my hands on Crawfie.

"All right, now it's time to talk," I said. "Begin right at the beginning and tell me the whole thing."

His mouth gaped helplessly. Under the magnifying lenses of his big spectacles his eyes squirmed back and forth across my face, like flies trying to get out of a bottle.

"Talk!" I yelled. I hit him hard. I may have knocked out a tooth or two; I know I cut my knuckles.

"Russell, Russell," he begged.

"Talk, or you won't have any teeth left."

"I—This—I was just picking up this package for a friend. I don't know what it is."

"Talk, don't lie." I slapped him some more. My hands were getting sore, so I could imagine how his face felt. He began to blubber.

"Russell, I—Look, I'll split with you. I got a good racket.

You know what it is—encouraging some wealthy boys to pay a little public relations fee, you know, so the public will keep on liking them."

"That's sure the only nice way you could put it."

"There's ten grand in this envelope. I'll split it with you."

"The hell you will. I'll take it. After I'm through with you. Where are you living now?"

"In my studio."

"And where's your studio, dummox?"

A flashlight beam blazed out of the darkness and stopped full on us. And as the light hit, somebody pulled the trigger of an automatic and held it back. A stream of lead came out of the dark.

I felt one bullet hit, but that was all. I was lucky they weren't better shots. I ducked under Crawfie's arm and rolled, pulling him over on top of me. We lay there flat on our backs for a minute. The shooting stopped and the light went out. Crawfie's breath was coming in agonized sobs.

"Okay, you slug," I whispered in his ear. "One sound from you and I'll shoot right through your back."

We stayed very still. I felt fairly safe, for the minute. I was protected against anything but a shot from point blank range. And I was lying on the money, so it was safe. I tried moving my arms and legs slightly, to see where I was hit, but nothing hurt me.

I was safe, but I was helpless. Lying on my back I couldn't hit the flat end of a moving van with a shot.

We were close to the back of the canteen. In an operation that must have taken fifteen minutes elapsed time I drew up my good leg, dug in my heel and shoved, then repeated and repeated until my head hit the wall of the canteen. All this time I was carrying Crawfie with me, on my stomach. The bastard had been eating too much for a long time.

Now I sat up, shoved back further, and sat with my back against the wall and Crawfie on my lap. So let them try to surprise me now! I got the guns both out. Two-gun Teed.

We must have made some noise sitting up. I began to have it figured now. They were out there just waiting to see if we'd been hit, before they tried to close in. They thought they'd given us long enough. The flashlight beam stabbed toward us again, and landed full on Crawfie's face.

"Don't, God, don't!" he screamed. "Don't shoot!"

They didn't. I did. I got both my guns pointed in the general direction of the flashlight just as it went out again, and pulled both triggers. I don't know which hand was lucky but there was a gargling cry of terror and pain from the darkness, and something hit the turf. Score one for Teed.

After that the silence got hard on the nerves. I don't know how long we sat. Crawfie was paralyzed. I was beginning to get a little paralyzed too—both my legs were going to sleep where he sat on them. I wriggled around to keep the blood flowing.

Maybe there had only been one. It would be nice to believe that. But I thought it was Irish Joe, and he never hunted alone. He had the little Indian with him, all the time. I didn't know whether I'd hit the Indian or Irish, but I figured it was one or the other.

The scheme wasn't as dumb as it had looked at first. They hadn't just sent Crawfie to collect the loot after Hamish left it. They'd been hidden somewhere, probably around the corner of a factory across the street, to see everything that happened.

They had been there to watch MacFaden drive up alone and leave the money, and be sure he wasn't followed or accompanied. Then they'd waited for Crawfie, following orders, to arrive on the scene by car and go in for the package.

What they hoped, of course, was that they'd be able to observe him get back into his car with the dough and drive away to some pre-arranged assembly point where they'd divvy it up afterward. And when Crawfie hadn't come back, they'd sneaked around to see what the hitch was.

From then on, the story was clear. They'd heard us talking and hoped to finish me off—and perhaps Crawfie too, they likely didn't care about him—with the first blast.

And they could—

Whop!

So help me, I hadn't heard a sound. And my ears were out in breeze waving like an angry elephant's. But here it was, a ton of brick landing on us from the side. By the weight, it was Irish Joe. By the amount of noise he'd made, he was awfully nimble on his feet.

Crawfie screamed again. This was his night for screaming. I lost one gun, but I clipped his head with the other to keep him still. He slumped off me and I was too busy for a while to drag him back.

Irish Joe had me by the neck, and was pounding at my head with a gun butt. It wasn't as bad as it sounds because I had one arm over my head and I was struggling so hard, his blows only glanced off me.

He bore down harder. I felt his fast, heavy breathing at my neck. I ducked my head and jerked it back into his face. I got a scalpful of teeth, but it hurt him more than me.

Crawfie was out of the way. I kicked my legs sideways, flattened out suddenly, dragged Irish Joe down with me before he could let go my neck, and then rolled. I ended up on top of him, but on my back and with arm still around my windpipe. He started to choke me.

I was helpless. I couldn't reach him with an arm or leg, and I couldn't get enough leverage to roll again.

Maybe there was a shell left in the gun. I stuck it under my back, against him, and pulled the trigger. There was a shot left all right. He went "Gahhh" in a gritted sob, and loosed his grip.

I rolled slowly off him and got painfully to my feet.

How were the mighty fallen! He looked about eight feet long, lying in the grass. He writhed a little. Then he raised his gun and shot at me. The bullet went past my ear.

I ducked under his gun and fell on him. His chest was sticky with blood. His lips were drawn back and his white teeth showed in a horrible grimace.

I worked on those white teeth with my gun. I thought about Priscilla, shot and lying in her own blood. I thought of her strangled in the hospital bed.

I didn't leave him one of those teeth.

I didn't leave him much of a face, either.

When I stood up, he was dead. He would have died anyway.

After I got my breath back I looked for Crawfie. He wasn't visible. I came around the corner of the canteen. I saw Crawfie crawling toward Riley. I sent a bullet to chase him.

Crawfie got to his feet and ran. When he got to Riley he reached for the door handle, and I shot again. I guess I fired too high; I didn't want to hit Riley. Anyway, I missed Crawfie but I scared him off. He dashed across Decarie, and I couldn't shoot again because there was some traffic. I followed him with my eyes and saw him run down the opposite side of the street and get into a car that was parked about two hundred yards down. I suppose it was Irish Joe's car. Crawfie drove away.

Irish Joe? The late Irish Joe. And how about the Indian?

I went back and found my flashlight where I'd dropped it. I swept the area for a minute and got the Indian in its beam. He was lying on his stomach. I went to him and turned him over with my foot. He was still wearing a filthy bandage on his face, but he wouldn't need it any more. His face wouldn't hurt him. He'd died about the way he deserved to die, with either two or three of my bullets in his body. It was good enough shooting to satisfy me.

I had one more thing to do. I located the packet of money back inside Irish Joe's body. It was intact.

Only one thing bothered me. I thought I'd been hit. Where?

I shone the flashlight on myself. My plaster cast was deeply creased by a bullet, and cracked right down the side.

That was interesting. Experimentally, I put my weight on that leg. The plaster cast split open and fell off. My leg buckled under me.

I fell on my nose and fainted.

Chapter Twenty-Two

I CAME TO. Lila was bending over me.

"My God, I thought you were shot too," she said.

"How did you get here?"

"I heard all the artillery go off. I waited until I couldn't stand the suspense any longer. Then I came over and you were all here. Jeez, the big boy's a mess."

"You better lie here until I go get the Morris. I'll bring it around to the curb here."

"Oh, no you won't. We have a better chariot here. Riley has at last come back to me."

I leaned on her and finally managed to make it to the Riley. This time my leg hurt an awful lot worse than when I first broke it.

Then I went through the same routine all over again.

After we got to the hospital, and waited an hour for Danny Moore—he took his time coming—I at last got another cast on the leg. All this time I hadn't made any phone calls. If I had to have a broken leg repaired, other people could wait for information.

Danny said, "This is getting to be a habit with you."

"Sure."

"Everything the same. Same hour of the morning, so I lose most of my night's sleep. Same client—"

"Same broken leg," I said. "At least you don't have to x-ray it this time."

"But different girl."

"Oh, definitely," I said. "No more casual pick-ups. I'm a reformed character. This is my mistress."

Danny laughed. Lila slapped my face—just for effect. I

felt the slap. It reminded me I hadn't had anything to drink for a good six hours.

So two men carried me back out to Riley, and Lila drove home and supported me in, and I drank four ounces of rye. That didn't seem enough under the circumstances, and I had a second shot. Then I said, "What time is it?"

"About four a.m."

"I better do some phoning."

I called Framboise first, and it was a quiet night so I found him at headquarters. I told him my story and it wasn't a quiet night, not for him, not any more.

"W'ere?" he asked.

I told him. He shot a squad off to collect bodies.

"Were t'ey the killers? T'e brains behind t'e whole racket? W'y did you shoot t'em?"

"Because they were shooting at me. No, they aren't the answer to the whole case. For one thing, Crawfie Foster is still on the loose. But it's beginning to come clear."

"W'at is clear? Not'ing is clear to me *à ce moment*."

"Well, I know why Wales was shot," I said. "Also, I know the photos were designed for blackmail. That kills your theory, thank God, because it was more trouble than it was worth."

"T'anks. W'at else you know?"

"All I know besides that is what I don't know. You follow me, I hope?"

"Almos'. Go on."

"I don't know who was the third partner in the gambling. He's the key to the business. He and Crawfie."

"W'ere is Crawfie?"

"That's my next assignment. Stay on duty, even if you have to work overtime after eight a.m. I have ideas. I'll call you back."

He protested, but not too hard. He was going to have a few busy hours processing what I'd given him already—in the way of information, and in the way of corpses. He made me promise to call him by nine, even if there was nothing new, and hung up.

I got Hamish MacFaden's number from the book, and called. I expected I'd have to wade through two or three footmen and then a butler, but Hamish was nervous. He'd been waiting for a call. He answered himself, before the phone finished ringing the first time.

"Be of good cheer," I said.

"What happened?"

"People came to collect your money. Now the morgue wagon is going out to collect them."

"Did—did you have to kill to protect me?"

"No, to protect myself. These types had it coming. By the way, I've got your money. I'll bring it around in the morning."

"You've got a wad of old newspaper. I trusted you implicitly."

"Thanks," I said. "The cheque I get in the morning better not be written in vanishing ink."

"It isn't. Am I safe now?"

"Almost."

"Hell! What do you mean?"

"The guy who took the pictures got away. He's only a small cog, though. He won't try anything. Besides, I'm going to pick him up. Tell me some things."

"Certainly. Anything."

"Who else that you know is being blackmailed?"

"Ah—"

"Come on. This is important. This is your skin."

"A few people have talked to me in confidence. In strict confidence.

"I'm very strict. Spill."

"All right. Pierre Esperent, head of Consolidated Hydro-Electric; Carl Mocklin, of Mocklin and Mocklin, the brokers; and Arthur Patter, president of the Ontario Bank."

"That all?"

"That's all I've heard of. The story is the same in each case. They've gambled in that Sherbrooke Street place, at one time or another, and they all got pictures and letters in the mail. Each was told to go to the Decarie canteen on a different night."

"I wish you'd told me this before."

"You didn't ask me."

"Okay, okay," I said wearily. "I'll call you back. Tomorrow, I hope. I'm going to crack this thing."

"Good luck."

"Good night."

Lila had made coffee, wonderful coffee. We sat around and drank it. Lila said she was sleepy.

"And I'm damned if I want to sleep on half a couch," she said.

"Okay. You can have the whole couch. I'll use the bed."

"Yeah?"

"Yeah. Remember, my cast is still wet."

It was five o'clock. The sleep we had was worse than nothing at all. I got up with the alarm jangling my ears, at eight. I tried to get Lila on her feet, but that proved impossible until I'd made coffee and waved a cup under her nose. While she dressed I organized more breakfast, and then we ate.

"Now what do we do?" she wanted to know.

"Go to the Redpath Library."

"It's too nice a day for that. Why don't we go for a drive in the country, if you're just trying to forget the case."

"I'm not trying to forget, I'm trying to solve it. Come on, you're still the chauffeur."

We went to the library and I asked for the latest Canadian *Who's Who*. Lila wandered off to the Periodicals room and amused herself while I studied the book. It gave me the clues I was looking for. I collected her and stumped back to Riley.

"Let's find a phone booth. I think I've got it, but I'll need some help."

We stopped in a coffee shop, and I called MacArnold.

"Greetings. Lovely morning to be alive."

"Yes," he agreed, "if you're asleep. What do you want?"

"Just thought I'd tell you who I killed last night. Irish Joe and his Indian friend."

"Good God! Does that wind up the case? How did you do it? Did you get hurt yourself? Is Framboise going to arrest you?"

"It doesn't wind up the case. I caught them out in the country where they were trying to pick up blackmail money Hamish MacFaden had left for them. I didn't get shot except in my cast, and Framboise is leaving me alone because he believes it was self-defense."

"They were trying to blackmail MacFaden, were they? Holy gee, a lot happens when I turn my back. I thought you were going to phone me if anything broke?"

"I was working it on the basis of a personal grudge, last night. I didn't want any help. I wanted to do it all myself. You see—yesterday afternoon, just after I left you and Montgomery, they killed Priscilla."

"Aw, no!"

"Crept into her hospital room and strangled her. I was too hit by it even to want to call you."

"Who? Who did it?"

"I wish I knew. One of the mob, of course. I didn't know what to do. I wanted to manufacture a few corpses, but I couldn't get my hands on anyone. Then I had luck. MacFaden called and told me where he was leaving the money—so I just went there and waited."

"How does the case stack up now?"

"Crawfie got away from me again, I was so busy shooting the other two. I've got to find him, and I've got to get the name of the third gambling partner from him. When I do that, we'll be through."

"How are you going to find Crawfie?"

"I have no idea." I told him of the conclusions Lila and I had reached regarding the photos. "I need some help," I went on. "If Montgomery is still sick of his office job, bring him along with you. Meet me in an hour, just before noon, at the corner of Beaver Hall Hill and La Gauchetiere."

"And what will we find?"

"If we're lucky, we're going to discover where those pictures were actually taken."

Lila and I filled in the hour drinking coffee slowly. Then we got into Riley and she drove him down Beaver Hall and parked just around the corner on La Gauchetiere. A few minutes later, MacArnold and Montgomery got out of a taxi a few feet away from us. I called to them, and they came over.

"I hear you've been busy," Montgomery said.

"A little bit. What did you two do?"

"I don't know what MacArnold did. After we left your place, I dropped him off, and went home and died. After one big hot bath and one large dinner, I wouldn't have gone looking for my brother's murderer. I slept until Mac called me this morning."

MacArnold said, "I picked a great night to go back to the paper. Hatch nabbed me when I came in, told me to leave a portrait of myself with him when I next went on an outside assignment, so he'd be able to remember what I looked like.

Then he stuck me on rewrite for eight solid hours. There were three fires and a large hold-up last night, and I haven't worked so hard since I was a cub. And I've only had three hours' sleep, so don't smile at me. What do we do?"

"You guys heeled?"

"No," they said.

I pulled my spare gun—Hanwood's gun—out of my jacket pocket and gave it to MacArnold. "Here. This time, no slip-ups," I said.

"You know anything about these things, Jimmy?" MacArnold asked, eyeing the automatic suspiciously. "I'm not sure I want to try using—"

"I'll take it, if you want," Montgomery said casually.

"No, you're the runner of the crowd," I said quickly. "If we flush Crawfie out and he tries to fade, I want you placed to chase him. I can't run with this leg, and Mac's too old and beery."

MacArnold shrugged and put the gun gingerly in his pocket. "Okay. What's the program?"

"Come on." I got out of Riley. "You stay here," I warned Lila. "There isn't likely to be bloodshed, but there won't be much to see either. Keep the motor running. We may need the car in a hurry."

I couldn't really think of any reason why we might need the car, but it satisfied Lila. She started the engine and sat.

MacArnold, Montgomery and I rounded the corner onto Beaver Hall Hill. We walked up the street a few yards until we were at the front steps of the St. Stephen Club. Traffic on the sidewalk was fairly thick, with an average of about one sedate character every fifteen seconds trotting into the club to be liquored and fed.

"All right," I said. "We now spread out. Jimmy, go up to the next store and stay out of sight in the entry. Mac, go back down the hill a bit and get behind the glass door of that restaurant on the corner. I'll stay here at the side of the St. Stephen Club steps. Know what to watch for?"

"Well, I'm damned!" MacArnold said. "So this was the set-up?"

"I hope so. Don't expect anything to happen for a little while. Watch carefully, as these head office-boys start coming out from lunch."

"How did you guess?"

"If I'm right, I'll tell you. We may draw a blank. On the other hand—well, watch carefully."

"For what?" Montgomery asked, puzzled.

"See those three buildings across the street. The first one is yours, the second mine, and the third Mac's. You won't see much, if anything. But concentrate on the second-storey windows. Look for anything suspicious, and whistle if you see it."

We took up our positions. We waited. It was hot.

Maybe I was wrong. Maybe it was a screwy idea. There sure as hell wasn't anything going on in the second storey of the building I'd picked to watch.

The sun slanted down and picked me out of the shadows beside the steps. I was back in as far as I could get. I got hotter.

Men who had finished their lunches started coming out of the Club. And nothing happened across the street.

Maybe I'd been seen. Maybe we'd all been seen.

I took a casual gander down the streets at MacArnold's building. Nothing. I looked up at Montgomery's.

One of the second-storey windows was open. It hadn't been open before. Behind it was blackness.

I left the shelter of the steps, keeping my head low and moving at a hop almost as rapid as a run. I went straight across Beaver Hall Hill, at peril of my life, making three cab drivers stand on their brakes. I looked back. MacArnold was standing at the far curb, and as I watched he began to dodge across. Jimmy Montgomery seemed to be daydreaming, but then he saw me, started, and ran for the street.

I led the way. There was a dingy tailor shop on the ground floor of the building. Beside its window, a door evidently gave on a stairway to the upper floors. "This was your building!" I accused Montgomery.

"I didn't see anything," he protested.

"Mac, you and I'll go up. Jimmy can wait here."

We went up the stairs as quietly as possible; I could have used a foam-rubber pad on the bottom of my cast, but I picked it up and set it down very gently. On the second floor front there were two doors. The one on the left was the one we wanted.

I went to it and listened. I didn't hear a sound.

I tried the knob. It was locked. I went back a few steps to consult with MacArnold.

"We'll have to break it down. I think Crawfie's in there. I hope he's alone."

"You break down the door and we'll see."

"How can I break it down? I can't get a run with this cast."

"So you want I should be the target?"

"Oh, never mind. Have your gun ready."

I stood about two feet from the door. I balanced myself carefully on the cast, lifted my other foot and smashed the door.

Luckily, the wood was old and rotten. I hit the door just below the knob, and the latch cracked.

Everything was fine, except I was flat on my face inside the room.

Chapter Twenty-Three

THERE WAS A STARTLED YELL.

My strongest desire was to draw my gun and get into position to defend myself. I ducked my hand inside my jacket and got my fingers around the butt, and that was all. I was lying on my holster.

It was all right, though. Crawfie was alone in the room. He was standing a little back from the window, beside a camera that sat on a solid tripod and sported one of the biggest telescopic lenses I ever saw.

Crawfie was what had yelled when the door broke. He'd been settled in here for weeks from the look of the junk accumulated around the bare room, and probably he'd felt perfectly safe and secure from discovery. The room was large and square, and held all the equipment a photographer would want to do delicate work. In one corner I saw an enlarger—he'd need that for making his fake prints—and rough tables along the walls held his papers and trays of solution. There was a cot against the other wall, and a small electric hot plate sitting on a chair.

Crawfie was goggling at me. He'd been completely surprised; had been concentrating so hard on his work that he hadn't seen us move around down on the sidewalk, hadn't heard us come up to his door. Now I rolled off my gun and pulled it out. "Okay, no smart tricks," I directed.

I got slowly up onto my foot and my cast and limped over to him. He gazed petrified at the gun. He quaked. I thought his big horn-rimmed glasses would shake right off his fat nose.

"MacArnold, we've caught it," I called. "Go get Jimmy."

I gestured with the gun. Crawfie jumped as if the gun was a red hot rod prodding him.

"Go sit on your bed, slug. Don't try to run."

He shook his head violently. He trotted to the cot and flopped down on it. Mac and Montgomery came in.

"It's all over but the shooting," I said. "Maybe there won't even be any shooting now. Mac, go get to a telephone and have Framboise come up here. I told him to stay at headquarters until I got in touch with him."

I went to the camera and squinted through its viewfinder. The lens was trained directly on the front door of the St. Stephen Club. As I looked, a man came out the door. He was framed in the viewfinder, in the instant of putting on his hat before he stepped down to the street, neatly as a screen close-up frames the star's gorgeous puss.

"This is it," I said again. "Okay, Crawfie. Any time you want to talk—"

"How did you know this was the place to look?" Jimmy asked.

"Simple enough. MacFaden gave me the names of a few others who'd been blackmailed. All I had to figure out was where they'd all meet, besides in the gambling apartment. *Who's Who* told me they were all members of the St. Stephen."

"Nice deducing."

"It wasn't that hard. This was the only club they all had in common. Once we'd tumbled to the fact that the photos were fakes, it followed through easily."

Montgomery was poking around the photographic, as opposed to the living, side of the room. "He's got a really complete shop set up here. Oh—oh. Look."

He held up a sheaf of enlargements. There were about a dozen. They were all enlarged prints of a single shot—a shot of the doorway of apartment sixteen.

"Okay, Crawfie. We know what you've been doing," I said. "We know why too. All we want to know is who is in it with you."

Crawfie found his tongue. "I—I was working with Irish Joe and his body guard," he said. "The two who were with me last night, out on Decarie."

"Yeah, sure." I went close to him and looked down. I swung my gun loosely, meaningfully in my hand. "You heard from them since last night? No. I'll tell you why—I killed them. But here you are, back in business this morning. Who told you to carry on with the job, Crawfie?"

"I—"

"Who else is in it? Come on."

He began to sob. "Nobody. Nobody, honest, Russell. I'm working for myself now. I wanted to get a few more shots to collect get-away money, and—"

"So you're the only one left, are you? You're the one who will take the rap for the Chesterley killing then. And the Wales shooting. And Priscilla Dover's death."

I tapped him on the cheek with the side of the gun, not enough to knock him over but enough to make an angry red mark. "Why did Priscilla have to die, Crawfie? How did she tumble?"

"She—"

He hesitated. That was a big mistake for him to make. I put the gun away and clipped him twice, once each way with my open hand. His teeth cut his lips. "Come on," I said. "Only God could save you now, and I doubt if he's interested in you. Sing."

He controlled his sobbing enough to talk. The tears dried in streaks on his pudgy, pasty face. "I had to have paper and supplies here. I phoned up my supplier and gave him a change of address. Priscilla was smart. She figured that out and checked with him. Then she came here one morning."

"And you let her in?"

"There's a bathroom down the hall. I'd gone in there and left this door unlocked for a minute. When I came back, she was in the room. She tried to pretend she hadn't tumbled to anything—just bawled me out for skipping without paying her, and asked for her salary. I stalled. When she left, I found one of the shots was missing."

"So you followed her to her home and shot her."

"No, no." He started to cry again.

"Come on, you tub of lard, before I begin kicking you with this plaster cast. Who shot her?"

He looked wildly around the room. His eyes picked up Montgomery, lounging against a table near the other wall. He looked at me. He saw I'd put my gun away.

Before I could realize what was happening, his hand darted under the pillow on the cot and came out with a small, short-snouted revolver.

"Hands up!" he screamed, just like the bad man in a Wild West movie.

The last thing I'd expected was that Crawfie would have a gun. I couldn't believe my eyes. I expected him to pull the trigger, when the cylinder of the gun would snap apart and reveal a flame for lighting cigarettes.

But no, it was a real gun.

I put my hands up. If the unbelievable could happen—if Crawfie had a gun—he might be desperate enough to use it.

"Don't argue with him," I said quietly to Montgomery. "He can't get away. MacArnold would stop him downstairs, and Framboise is probably down there now anyway."

Crawfie hauled his fat, sloppy body off the cot. "Back up!" he ordered me, and I shuffled away from him.

He waddled sideways to the door. He kept the gun moving from me to Montgomery, and his eyes carefully on us.

Montgomery yelled, "Okay, MacArnold. *Now!*"

Crawfie was an amateur, of course. He didn't shoot us first, then turn to see what was behind him. He just turned.

Montgomery dived for his legs and brought him crashing down. Then for a minute they were swarming all over each other. Crawfie was panting and screaming curses and lashing at Montgomery with the gun; Jimmy stopped one or two hard lashes, and then got it in both hands.

They were a mass of heaving flesh and cloth on the floor, the gun buried somewhere in the mass. Montgomery heaved hard, got one knee loose and drove it into Crawfie's soft and flabby stomach.

With reflex action, as his wind burst out of his body, Crawfie's finger tightened on the trigger. There was a roar. And with the roar, both of them collapsed.

Chapter Twenty-Four

Footsteps pounded on the stairs. MacArnold dashed into the room with Framboise at his heels. They skidded to a stop before the prone bodies.

"Oh, Goddamn!" I sobbed.

Framboise bent quickly and pried Montgomery away from Crawfie. As he was pulled away, Jimmy shook himself and straightened his arms and legs.

Crawfie didn't shake himself. And someone would have to straighten his arms and legs for him when they got him to the morgue. The gun had been flat against his chest, pointed up toward his head, when he pulled the trigger. The bullet had entered his head just underneath his chin and torn his face up so badly all you could recognize were his spectacles.

" 'Ow did t'is happen?" Framboise roared.

Montgomery gasped and got his breath. "Little scrap."

I stumped over and stood looking down at Crawfie. He was not pretty to look at, but I studied him as though he held the answer to my problems. And he did. Only he wasn't talking.

"Oh, Goddamn," I said bitterly again, "there went our last chance to clean up the case. Now we'll never know."

"Never know what?"

"Who killed Chesterley, Wales, Priscilla Dover. Crawfie didn't do all that by himself, believe me. He wasn't bright enough. He was directed—and by a person unknown, who's going to get away with murder."

"*Torieu*, explain yourself completely!" Framboise howled.

"Sure," I said. "Just listen. I've already told you there were three partners in the gambling apartment—Chesterley before he died, Irish Joe, and a person unknown. Now this unknown person wasn't Crawfie. Why?

"First of all, the third partner found out I was interested in the case, and sent Irish Joe and his sap-swinger to beat me up. Crawfie had no way of knowing I was in the case. Second, the third partner knew Priscilla was going to communicate Crawfie's whereabouts to me—therefore she was dangerous and had to be shot. Crawfie didn't know that. Third—"

"Wait a minute!" MacArnold yelled.

Something had come over him. He was trembling, either with excitement or with rage. He dragged the gun I'd given him from his pocket.

MacArnold pointed the gun squarely at Montgomery.

He was so excited the words fairly tobogganed out of his mouth. The gun in his hand shook. But it kept pointing at Jim.

MacArnold said, "How dumb can we all be? What do we know about this jerk? The first any of us ever heard of him was when he found Chesterley's body. That was a nice touch, all right. Kill a guy you have no connection with at all, and then just to be doubly safe, find the corpse."

Montgomery's lips tightened and his hands formed themselves into fists and came out from his sides in a gesture of tense rage. "Take it easy," he warned. "You're going to be sorry."

"Oh, no I'm not. I'm the one with the gun for a change. Who was sitting right beside me when I first proposed to Teed that he look for Chesterley's killer? You were. Who was with Teed the evening Priscilla came to him, scared to death, and said she'd tell him about Crawfie? And that's not all. Teed and I were together when Wales was killed. But you—you were somewhere in the immediate neighborhood. Where? Behind Wales, firing a shot into him?"

A dull purple-red had suffused Montgomery's face. I never saw a man so mad, or going to such pains to hold himself in. "You talk too much, Junior!" he growled.

"Maybe. I wish I wasn't talking too late. Too late to save Chesterley, Wales and Priscilla from you. Yes, and even little Crawfie, the poor misguided bastard. It looked like Crawfie was going to talk, didn't it? Well, you made sure he'd never tell us anything. You—"

Montgomery had had enough. He took a step.

"Stand back!" MacArnold screeched.

It was too late for that. Montgomery kicked, and the gun sailed neatly out of MacArnold's hand, arched through the air, and was fielded by Montgomery with a neat high catch.

Montgomery had his teeth clenched so tightly he could hardly grit his words through them. "Framboise," he asked, "you don't believe this, do you?"

"Put t'at gun away, an' I tell w'at I believe."

"Oh, no. Nobody's pulling any more fancy accusations on me. I'm just going for a little walk and let you all cool off. When I see in the papers you've really found out who's guilty, I'll show up again. Meantime don't send anybody to look for me. Because I'm keeping this,"—he flourished the gun—"and I know how to use it a lot better than MacArnold does."

He left the room. We heard him running down the stairs.

"*Sacrement!* I should 'ave brought some men wit' me," Framboise cursed. He and MacArnold dashed for the open window.

"There he goes—crossing the street!" MacArnold shouted. "You've got your gun, Framboise! Wing him."

Framboise shook his head. "In a crowded street? Too dangerous. Leave 'im. 'E won't get far."

"Relax, both of you," I said.

"Yeah?" MacArnold faced me angrily. "I notice you didn't try to stop him. You've still got a gun too. What's the matter?"

"I like the guy."

"Oh, fine. Last night you're itching to get your mitts on the guy who killed Priscilla. Today you like Montgomery, so you let him wander safely away."

"Sure. And I'm still itching to get the guy who killed Priscilla. And I will. As for Montgomery being the guy—I could make out as good a case against you as you made against him."

"Bull roar," MacArnold said belligerently.

"Who's been in on the case all the way along?" I asked pointedly. "Who was right in there with me, keeping up with progress of all my investigations? That could have been so you'd know just what moves to make next yourself."

"Why, you ungrateful bastard!" MacArnold roared. "Who pointed out the connection between Crawfie and the rest of the case? Who located the gambling apartment for you? Who told you Chesterley was one of its owners?" He came toward me. Now it was his turn to get enraged, the innocent and wrongly-accused man.

"Careful, careful," I said. "Like you just reminded me, I still have my gun."

"All t'is talk is getting us nowhere," Framboise chimed in. "I am tired of t'is nonsense. Come. We're going down to 'eadquarters toget'er and straighten t'is t'ing out."

"Sure," I agreed.

"Like hell we are," MacArnold snorted.

That was enough for Framboise. He drew his gun and stuck it in MacArnold's back. "So? You knew so much about Chesterley. So much about t'e gambling hapartment.

Me, I t'ink you can hexplain to us 'ow you knew so much. Come."

"You two go right ahead," I said. "I'll follow in the Riley."

MacArnold was speechless with rage. Framboise nudged him down the stairs with the gun. I stumped along after them. At the street, Framboise pushed Mac into the back seat of the police car, got in with him, and the driver started away with them.

I needed a little more time.

I went to the Riley. "Where to?" Lila asked.

"Home," I said. "And drive like you have a siren on this thing."

"What are you looking for now?"

"The usual. Trouble. But I figure this will be the last bit of it."

Chapter Twenty-Five

I LIMPED ALONG the corridor toward my apartment door. It was too early in the day for the lights to be on, but not much sunlight penetrated the place. There were heavy shadows.

Emerging from these, as I approached my door, was a smart figure. Of a woman.

"The trouble kid herself," I said.

"I came back. I said I would come back."

"This is a hell of a time to come, Elena. I gave you to Hanwood last night. He wanted to kill me so you'd stop seeing me."

"Oh."

"Does he know you came here again?"

"No," she said.

"Yes!" snarled Hanwood.

He emerged from the shadows beside Mrs. MacEchran's door. He had sneaked in there somehow without Elena seeing him; she gasped as he spoke.

Of course he had a gun in his hand. And there was on his face the expression of a man who has stood all he can stand. As far as Hanwood was concerned, the last straw had been laid on his back. He was going to reclaim Elena if he had to hang for it.

I unlocked my door. "Come in, come in," I said. "This would make such a mess in the hall. You too, Elena. Or would you sooner wait here for the winner?"

Hanwood laughed. "The winner? A naive way to put it, Teed. As though we were going to duel."

"We are, Hanwood." I swung on him, my gun in my hand. "You're careless, Paul," I said. "Just because I wasn't carrying a gun when you braced me in the hall before, you think I'm always unarmed? You think I never learn? Come in. And you'd better keep your eyes on this gun—on my trigger finger. Because I'm watching yours. The first sign of nervousness and I let fly."

He was sweating. He didn't mind shooting in cold blood. He didn't relish a gun fight, though. He wasn't that sure of his aim.

I backed through my hallway and into the living room. My gun never wavered from his chest. He followed at a respectful distance. He wasn't watching me at all. His eyes were on my gun. I had him worried.

Elena followed on behind, staring, still.

We planted ourselves across the living room from each other, the big rug between us.

"The time has come," I said. "The end of the road, and all that. This was a fine routine, Paul, this jealousy angle. You wanted to kill me because I was stealing your girl. That was the only reason, was it? Wasn't there maybe a chance you were trying to put me out of the way because I was coming too close to you?"

He shifted uneasily. I jerked my gun up an inch, to show him how carefully I was watching, and he froze.

"I'll begin at the beginning. There was an apartment used for gambling, Paul. You knew about it because it was right across the hall from your front door. Apartment sixteen. It was run by three men—a tough yegg named Irish Joe, a guy named Chesterley who was respectable on the surface, and a third partner so respectable he never appeared.

"Now, the third partner was an expensive boy who needed an awful lot of money for living. His share of the apartment earnings, big as they were, were not enough. So he had a brain-wave. Why not take pictures of the important people who came to gamble? Then, somehow, get the police interested in the place so they would raid it. The pictures would then become a lot more valuable than the apartment had ever been.

"There was only one partner who didn't like this idea. Irish Joe had no reputation at all—if the place was raided, he could pull out and open up shop elsewhere. The silent third partner wouldn't be connected with the plan at all. But poor Chesterley was an established citizen; he'd be ruined if it became known he was a gambling club owner. All his friends would cut him—even his wife didn't know his business. So Chesterley objected to the plan. The stakes were so big this meant he had to be rubbed out.

"I figured out quite a while ago how Chesterley's killing happened to take place on the mountain. It wasn't because he liked taking lonely walks—he knew his way around too well for that. It was because he had a rendez-vous with the third partner up there. Not Irish Joe; Irish he could meet in the apartment any time. The third partner always stayed away from that place, and met the others in secret. So he met Chesterley on top of Mount Royal. He probably brought Irish along for a muscle man. And it was the last meeting Chesterley ever had with anyone."

"You're telling me all this because it amuses you?" Paul Hanwood demanded.

"Be patient," I said. "I'll continue my story. Crawfie Foster had been recruited as photographer by this time, and since it was a little dangerous to use apartment fifteen for that job he had doped out a way to snap men who had been observed at the club, and fake the negatives so they could be used for blackmail. Only one thing went wrong. Priscilla Dover was smart enough to follow Crawfie to his hiding-place. Too bad for Priscilla. When the third partner found she intended to tell me, he silenced her.

"Now everything was ready. A victim was picked. To have police raid the gambling joint was desirable. To have them come there and find a corpse, as well as gambling, doubled the return from the blackmail. So it was carefully staged. Someone watched Wales gambling. That was Crawfie. As Wales got ready to leave, Crawfie phoned the third partner. The third partner called the police to tell them about the body—remember, they got there before Wales was cold—and then was getting ready to shoot Wales. But there was a hitch."

"Very clever, Teed," he admitted. Maybe it was my imagination, but I thought his finger tightened on the trigger. Mine did likewise. But neither gun spoke.

I said, "When MacArnold and I came into your apartment you were about to step out and shoot Wales. You'd already called the cops. There was no time to lose—and there we were. Lucky there was an alternate plan. Lucky someone else was standing ready with a gun. I could be wrong, but I'd say it was Crawfie."

"I suppose the little weasel told you," Hanwood burst out. "I suppose he told you all this—even admitted to murder. The white-livered little—"

"Never mind him. He's dead. He died before he could talk. But thanks for the confirmation. You see, you were the only one except MacArnold, Montgomery and myself who could have guessed when I first came into the case. You were there in the Alamo Club when Priscilla told me she'd found Crawfie. You were coming out to the canteen on Decarie for a meeting with Crawfie and Irish Joe, the night I followed them there and got my leg broken. You've been around all the time—and operating against me with a good screen. You weren't trying to stop my work on the case—oh, no.

You were trying to keep me away from Elena. Well, I guess that's all, Hanwood. That's the end for you. You bludgeoned Chesterley while Irish Joe held his arms. You shot Priscilla while she slept and then strangled her while she lay sick and weak on a hospital bed. How do you like this for a change? Irish Joe and Crawfie are gone. They won't help you, won't do your killing for you. How do you like facing an opponent with a gun?

"I'm going to count to three and then fire. You fire whenever you're ready, Paul. I'm not afraid of your aim."

There was a scream and a flashing body in front of me, and Elena was hanging onto my arm. "No, no!" she screamed. "There's been enough killing. I can't stand it. I can't—"

A gun roared. He hadn't waited for Elena to get clear. And in shooting, he had defeated his own purpose. I wasn't touched.

But Elena's voice stopped in a choking whisper, and she collapsed to the floor. And with her, she dragged in a death grip my gun-hand and my gun.

He laughed. "Now it is all over, Teed. Really all over."

He raised his gun and aimed carefully for my heart.

And behind him, a beer bottle lifted higher and higher, and then with the sickening *splat* of a hammer cracking a cocoanut came down to split his skull.

"Thanks, Lila," I said.

I stumped across the floor to him. I turned him face-upward with my foot. He was dead.

"Is Elena—?"

"Yeah."

"A fine conclusion."

"Almost. Only two more things to do."

"Like what?"

"Phone Framboise," I said. "But first this." I got my gun

from beside Elena's body. Then I came over to where he lay on the floor.

"That for Chesterley," I said, and shot. "That for Wales." I shot again.

Then I pointed the gun at his face and emptied the rest of the clip. "That," I said, "for Priscilla."

Out in the corridor a woman screamed. I knew who it was. It was Mrs. MacEchran.

"Police! Help, police!" she yelled.

"Quiet, you old washerwoman!" I roared.

Lila came to me and put her hand on my arm. "There's only one way to get away from her. Away from the whole mess. Let's take your ten thousand dollars and go to—to Bermuda."

THE END